Praise for *The River Between Hearts*

"A shimmering, breathtaking read! *The River Between Hearts* has everything I hope for in a great middle grade novel: A spirited heroine with a voice that leaps off the page, a scenic setting I want to spend time in, vivid characters, adventure, swift page-turning chapters, and heart—this book positively sparkles with emotion. Fans of Kate DiCamillo will be delighted by the wonderful tale that Heather Mateus Sappenfield has crafted!"

—Todd Mitchell, *The Last Panther*, Nautilus Book Award and Colorado Book Award Winner

"Rill is determined to stay exactly the same. Everyone and everything around her is changing and growing up. But despite the fact that 5th grade is around the corner and "popular and liking" are all anyone can talk about, Rill won't budge. In an attempt to escape the ever-changing landscape around her, she visits her old hideaway, Fort Kruse. She expects the old photos and old drawings that will painfully attempt to bring back unwanted memories, but she does not expect to find someone hiding out in the Fort. A chance encounter of two lives in upheaval leads to a beautiful story of friendship, healing, and a cemented belief that people are not things. Sappenfield does a beautiful job at tackling important issues for middle grade students to grasp! Highly recommend!"

—Sarah Hopkins, Bookseller, Bookworm of Edwards

"Heather Mateus Sappenfield's *The River Between Hearts* is a beautiful young MG that hits all the right notes: a strong heroine who's dealing with all the changes of growing up, and has a broken heart that needs mending. This story has lots of heart, a beautiful setting, and a spirited, sweet voice make the words come alive. Perfect for fans of Leslie Connor's *A Home for Goddesses and Dogs* and Laurel Snyder's *My Jasper June*. The Colorado setting shines and carries you away. *The River Between Hearts* is a middle-grade novel not to be missed!"

—Fleur Bradley, MG author of *Midnight at the Barclay Hotel*, NPR Best Book of 2020

"*The River Between Hearts* is a beautifully written story about friendship and acceptance. Rill and Perla are heading into summer vacation dealing with their own grief and loss. They learn, 'The best adventures…true ones…test you and teach you about yourself.' Heather Mateus Sappenfield does a wonderful job describing the impact of immigration on children in resort communities and I look forward to sharing this novel with my students."

—Beth Cooney, Lead Literacy Teacher, Edwards Elementary School

"Rill and Perla may be very different, but the adventure that awaits them this summer will prove the opposite. The two have to repair hearts that do not know about language, social class, or race, yet the friendship that unites them will be stronger. *The River Between Hearts* is a clear example of what an intercultural friendship means, and the mental health of a child at ten years of age, and the healing process that entails them. The river that took what they want the most will be the same one that will unite them in the fight to find the best in each other, in the fight to find themselves."

—Rocio Garcia-Roa, Technical Services Specialist, Eagle Valley Library District

**Other Books by
Heather Mateus Sappenfield**

Lyrics for Rock Stars: Stories

Life at the Speed of Us

The View from Who I Was

THE RIVER BETWEEN HEARTS

Heather Mateus Sappenfield

Fitzroy Books

Published by Fitzroy Books
An imprint of
Regal House Publishing, LLC
Raleigh, NC 27587
All rights reserved

https://fitzroybooks.com

Printed in the United States of America

ISBN -13 (paperback): 9781646032068
ISBN -13 (epub): 9781646032075
Library of Congress Control Number: 2021936001

Interior and cover design by Lafayette & Greene
Cover images © by C.B. Royal

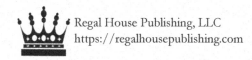

Regal House Publishing, LLC
https://regalhousepublishing.com

Printed in the United States of America

For Norma
and compassion

To live in hearts we leave behind
Is not to die.

— Thomas Campbell, 1777-1844, "Hallowed Ground"

1

My tree house, Fort Kruse, wasn't far from home if you had wings. But if you were stuck on the ground, stubby cliffs blocked the way, so the trail looped around. Behind me the creek nagged *Rill! Rill! Rill!*, making me mad enough to spit. Rosebushes scratched my arms and legs, and spiderwebs stuck to my face. Clifford shot between my shins, making me scream like a girl, which I guess was all right, because I am one. But still.

"GIVE ME A BREAK!" I shouted at that crazy cat. Really, though, I was shouting at the whole danged world.

And then, there I was at Fort Kruse.

I'd forgot how much I loved its cheery golden color. Forgot the roof was the big gray plastic one off our playhouse from when Eddy and me were little. Forgot we'd painted the shutters sky blue. The flag with the *K* Mom had sewn snapped on the breeze. At the ladder I peered up. Handprints—Eddy's, Mom's, Dad's, and mine—waved from the floor's underneath. I looked down at my sneakers, swallowing, because those hands seemed so happy to see me.

I climbed the rungs and nudged up the trap door, lifting it higher, higher, till it fell, banging against the floor. I shuffled to a window and unhooked its shutters. Sunshine exploded across the hammock, table, and one stump chair. The other stump chair lay on its side, against the wall from when I'd kicked it last September. There was the shelf with our family photo and my four drawings hanging on the walls. Everything was just how I'd left it. Except the air. *That* seemed better, cleaner.

I dragged the stump chair back to the table and walked up

the sunbeam to look out the window. Dad always called this The Eagle's View.

I opened the next set of shutters and took in the view from there. Opening the last set, I looked out on home. Our company's building reminded me of a big brown pencil box, except with a green metal roof for a lid. Off its back corner, the snowmobiles for winter tours were parked in rows. Off its other corner, bright blue river rafts were stacked on the one trailer that hadn't been hauled away by a van stuffed with guests. I could also see the back side of the Kruse Whitewater Adventures sign at the two-lane highway, the dirt road in, and the bridge across the creek. I filled my chest with the smells of trees and plants and animals busting awake after the long winter.

At a ruckus on the ladder, I flinched. Of course my slingshot was in my backpack against the opposite wall. Breathing fast, I watched a paw reach through the door, then another as Clifford clawed his way in, ears flat back from how hard he worked.

"Don't scare me like that!" I scolded.

"Meow," he replied like *I'll do whatever I please,* and he strode around, inspecting everything.

I plopped onto a stump chair, resting my elbows on my knees and my chin in my hands. Then I could *feel* our family photo staring down at me. Twisting around, I stared right back. I'd been nine in that photo: Rill Kruse, shortest person in third grade. A year and twenty-six days had gone by since Gus took it, and I'd been careful to stay *exactly* the same. I whispered to Dad, giant beside me up there, "Come home for my birthday, okay? Plea—"

I heard a swishy sound and froze. After a few seconds, there it was again. The third time my heart about stopped because I realized it was coming from the hammock.

2

Pretending to look out a window, I watched the hammock bulge. I felt for my whistle at my chest, but, of course, I'd thrown it away.

Sliding on my backpack, being super obvious, I said, "Come on, Clifford," same as when we left on our daily stroll to the mailbox. I climbed down the ladder, nervous clear to my fingers and toes, listening for whatever hid in the hammock to attack me. At the bottom I looked up. Clifford peered down.

"Meow?" he said, like *Seriously? You're leaving?*

"Clifford!" I whispered. "Come on!"

But he just stared with his Lifesaver-green eyes.

"Suit yourself!" I took off for home. After a few steps, though, I paused. Whatever was in that hammock might hurt Clifford. It might even eat him! "CLIFFORD!" I called, but he did not come.

Gritting my teeth, I slid off my pack and dug inside for my slingshot. Then I thought how the fort was actually pretty small, so I might not have enough room to shoot. I zipped my pack closed and searched around till I found a stick big and thick enough to swing, but also light enough to drag up the ladder.

Climbing the rungs, I cursed that cat. He was the whole reason I'd come there in the first place. Near the top I listened again. Was that...*purring?*

Inching my head through the doorway, I saw that something was *definitely* still swishing in the hammock. I listened again. That *was* purring, but I couldn't spot Clifford. The camouflage pattern made it hard to tell the shape of what hid inside, but it seemed *big.*

I stepped in, raising the stick, ready to swing, and took two slinky steps.

Nothing happened. The purring got louder. I slunk two steps closer.

Nothing happened. The purring got even louder. I slunk two steps more.

I cocked back the stick for a home run but stopped. If I clobbered that hammock, Clifford might get hurt. Plus, if he was purring, whatever hid in there obviously wasn't eating him. Still, my palms were slippery with sweat as I changed to a sword grip. Imagining Joyce saying, *Ready…go!* I jabbed, lightning fast.

The thing in the hammock screamed.

I screamed.

Clifford yowled as he and a body spilled onto the floor.

That cat zoomed to the far windowsill like a pufferfish with a broomstick tail. The body rolled onto its hands and knees. Her hair was black and tangly, but her eyes were even tanglier. Slow and careful, she stood up. She was only a bit taller than me and seemed about my same age. She wore jeans with a belt and a T-shirt that had *Los,* then two more words hidden in a wrinkle. Above that was a photo of four men, two of them holding guitars. For a minute that girl and I tried to murder each other with dirty looks. Then she shivered. Her chin lifted, all proud, and the shivering stopped.

Proud? About breaking into *my* fort? "GET OUTTA HERE!" I shouted.

Her hands shot up like she was under arrest and she started inching sideways, making for the trap door. Then she disappeared down the ladder.

I swooped over the doorway, just in time to see her skip the last rung and hit the ground sprinting. But she didn't head in the direction I expected. No, she ran deeper into the forest.

3

Blowing out a humongous breath, I let the stick clunk to the fort's floor. Sweat coated me, so to cool down I squirmed off my backpack.

I'd seen that girl before. At school. And then it came to me why: because of my ex-friend, Whitney.

Last year, just before winter break, Whitney and her popular friends had been standing in a clump in the hallway, crinkling their noses at a new student. *Popular* became a huge deal in fourth grade, by the way, and Whitney was the queen of *who* was popular and *who* wasn't. With what had happened in Fort Kruse, *I* definitely *wasn't*. Plus, it all seemed so *dumb*. And then boys started *liking* girls, and girls started *liking* boys. I swear, it was ridiculous because we'd known each other since kindergarten. I tried to ignore it all—to just stay me—but every time I turned around, there it was. I'd never been so glad for field day—school's last day—to come along. But of course, the popular girls, plus the girls who *wanted* to be popular, just stood around whispering and giggling. Not me: I won seven blue ribbons. Anyway, there they were, standing in the hall before lunch, looking at the very girl who'd spilled out of *my* hammock.

Concentrating on that memory, I moseyed over to the hammock and plopped in sideways, the way Eddy and I used to when we both wanted to lie there at once. I prickled, remembering the dirty look Whitney'd shot me that day, just as something rolled into my lap. Boy did I holler out of that hammock! Clifford watched like I was hilarious.

"Don't laugh!" I snapped at him. "This is all your fault anyway!"

Using the stick, I tugged back the hammock's edge and

spied a white plastic sack, the kind Mom and Joyce carried in from their shopping trips to the grocery store. Like it might bite, I lifted it out, set it on the table, and just stared at it because going through a stranger's stuff felt creepy. Still, I needed to find out about this girl who'd been hiding in *my* fort.

I pulled out another T-shirt with the same photo of the men. There was *Los* written below it again. The next word was *Padres*. But the last word? Was it *Can't*? I'd learned enough Spanish in school and listened to Joyce enough to know *los* meant "the" and *padres* meant "dads." The Dads Can't?

Next I pulled out a pair of jeans, a pair of underwear, a pair of nubbly socks, a hairbrush, three chewy granola bars, an empty water bottle, and a little white teddy bear with a stitched rectangle on its chest that was one-third green, one-third white, and one-third red. In the middle white third was a stitched brown bird with spread wings.

That empty sack drooped on the table like a tired balloon. The way its eight things spilled from it reminded me of when Eddy caught trout and cleaned out their guts in the creek. Something about that sack and its guts made me slump, feeling like I might never rise again.

As I stared at the girl's stuff, what Alissa said to Whitney that day at school came back to me: *Another one?* She'd said it real loud on purpose, and the girl had looked at Alissa with the same expression she'd given me here in the fort. But then Whitney did something that made me stare. She said, just as loud, *Shut up, Alissa!* and nodded to the girl like *Sorry.* Then she'd caught me watching. I remembered going over and over the way Whitney had scolded Alissa. I couldn't get over how rotten it must've made Alissa feel, but I'd never once thought about how that new girl might've felt. I didn't even know her name.

Clifford hopped into my lap, prancing back and forth, holding his tail so it tickled my face.

"Not now," I muttered. Still, my hand came to his back and he started to purr.

This girl sure seemed to be on the run. What things would I pack if *I* ran away? More food. Definitely more food. Then again, maybe there wasn't any food at home to take. Or maybe she didn't have time to pack food. Or maybe she ate all her food. Maybe the stuff in this bag really was like fish guts. Maybe she needed it to survive.

4

Do you ever break your own promises to yourself? I sure do.

Earlier that morning, I'd been eating my cereal at the kitchen table, telling my legs to stay put. But they wouldn't listen. Instead they drifted down the metal stairs, then alongside the building. Even though I thought *Go back! Go back!* they marched straight into the lobby. The vans with their raft trailers were rumbling away. My insides swayed, but I watched till the only thing left of them was dust.

"Uck!" Joyce stood behind the counter, gathering the guests' signed waiver forms. "That's a trout mouth! A frown that big? On the first official day of summer break? Hmm-mmm!"

Joyce had been our office manager and mechanic since before I was born. She and Mom had met way back in high school, and they always insisted that at first they'd hated each other. And I mean *hate* because one day they got in an actual *fistfight*. Then, when they served detention together, they became best friends, and they've taken care of each other ever since.

Everything Joyce said—in Spanish or English—ended with an exclamation point. She always wore a ponytail high on her head and a company tank top stretched across her chest. Her biceps looked like chicken drumsticks because she was an arm wrestler. Her trophies crowded the shelf behind her desk. Gold or silver, some had bodies from the waist up, some just the arms. All of them had two planted elbows with two right hands, gripped and ready.

Clifford rubbed against my shins.

"Have a grape!" She pointed at a glass bowl overflowing with them.

I could count on Joyce to have some kind of boring fruit in that bowl since she was always "staying lean," which meant drinking lots of water and eating grapes, apples, clementines, or bananas, instead of candy.

I took a seat on the stool, and an upside-down stack of waiver forms stared back at me. I looked at the scribbly date of the one on top: one year and thirteen days since Dad had left. Groaning, I hunched over till my forehead pressed the counter.

"Why don't you draw?"

I loved to draw. Dad was super good at it, so he'd taught me, and I drew stuff all the time. Just then, though, it sounded so boring that I groaned again.

"Hmm. Wanna pull?"

"Pull" meant arm-wrestle. Joyce had been coaching me since I was five in how to stand, rest my elbow on the special table she kept in the garage, and snap my wrist. How to surge my whole body forward lightning fast when the referee said, "Ready...go!" She called me a prodigy. "Prodigy" means a person who's a wonder at something. I'd pulled and beaten most of the guides. Joyce wanted me to practice on the guests. Especially the men. But Mom insisted it wasn't practical. "Bad for business," she'd say. Usually, pulling with Joyce cheered me up.

"Nah," I sighed, rolling my head till my cheek met the cool counter. On Joyce's bicep was a curlicue tattoo that read *Leo*. From down there, it was sideways. Actually, my *whole life* seemed sideways.

I wished Leo could help me the way he helped Joyce. When a problem with one of the company vans stumped her, he'd swing by from his mechanic shop. They'd stand in front of an engine, puzzling out its problem, the top of his head the same height as his name on her arm. They'd fix it, and he'd smile up at her, so proud. Lately, when this happened, his edges would blur and suddenly he'd be giant beside her. I'd rub my eyes till he shrank back tattoo-tall.

Clifford shot off the stool beside me and out the door.

"Ah, man!" I hopped down to follow. He trotted alongside the building, then zoomed across the meadow behind home.

"Clifford!" I called.

At its far side he turned back, calling, "Meow!" Then he started up the trail to Fort Kruse. That was bad. Because things with fangs, horns, or quills lived up there. Our Kruse Whitewater Adventures trash dumpster was bear proof. On summer nights the yips and yowls of coyotes drifted in my open window. Sometimes a moose grazed along the creek's marshy spots, and if it was a mom moose with a calf, it was double dangerous. Skunks, porcupines, and raccoons were always a worry. Worst of all—and maybe the scariest because I'd never seen or heard even a hint of one—were mountain lions. "Probably you've seen one and didn't even realize it!" Eddy warned, back when I was in third grade and he was in sixth. Back when he still talked to me. "Probably if you ever do see one, it'll be as it attacks! Probably you'll never even know it's coming! Just...*bam!*"

"Joyce!" I shouted. "I have to go chase my danged cat!"

"Not without your whistle!" she answered.

Rolling my eyes, I rushed up the stairs.

5

My room has two twin beds. Scooching on my belly till half of me was wedged under the one closest to the window, my fingers touched a strap. I grabbed and yanked, dragging dust balls into bright sunlight. I hadn't even *looked* at my red backpack in forever. I traded the backpack I used for school for my red one, and *that*, at least, felt good.

At my desk I dropped in my slingshot, a baggie of rocks I'd gathered for shooting, and *Chitty Chitty Bang Bang*. Crossing my fingers, I slid the pack on, hoping I wouldn't have to let out the straps since I hadn't worn it in so long. They were tight, but I left them alone.

Two danged whistles hung with the keys beside the screen door—mine on an orange cord and Eddy's on a brown cord. Ever since we were little, we'd been wearing them when we went into the forest. On account of all the animals mostly, but also for if something went wrong. Reaching for mine, I paused, thinking how I'd be in fifth grade next year. "No changing!" I scolded myself, and I put it on.

Joyce waited at the bottom of the stairs with a sandwich wrapped in foil, a little bag of potato chips, two bottles of water, and a bunch of grapes—leftovers from the lunches for the guests.

"I'm in a hurry!" I moaned.

"You never know!" Unzipping my backpack, she tucked the food inside. "Remember to drink! Hydration is key!"

I tore across the meadow. At its far side, I looked back and she shouted, "Find that *gato loco*!"

A little ways up the trail, Clifford sat, waiting. When I got close, he took off. "Clifford!" I scolded. "What the heck are you doing?" Around the next curve, there he sat. When I got close, he did it again.

Pretty quick, I was wiping off spider webs, all scratchy and itchy. For some reason I remembered Dad saying, *Eighth grade: that's when you'll become a teenager, that's when you can start working summers with us. Until then just be kids.* Since Eddy'd turned thirteen, he'd be working all summer. He was probably handing out paddles right that minute. Mom was probably laughing and talking in her guest voice. Gus was probably checking to make sure the rafts held air. And there *I* was, chasing after my stupid cat.

I thought how Whitney had bragged that she was going to Hawaii for the summer. Not to me, of course, but to Alissa. I pictured Whitney drinking from a coconut through a long straw, her hair in braids with those pink ribbons fluttering in an ocean breeze. I really did *not* want to think about her right then, but here's the thing: She lived in a house that was practically a castle, with a yard so pretty you hated to muss it up. She belonged to a pool with fluffy white towels and a stand that gave out awesome snacks. Best of all, she had Sir Charles's Shanty, a shiny black pony that she took lessons on twice a week and jumped in horse shows.

I hate swimming, so I never even got in the pool, but I ate a ton of ice cream bars. What I loved was riding lessons. I'd sit on the arena's top rail and watch Whitney sail along on Sir Charles. Her blonde braids with their pink ribbons would stream behind her black velvet cap like a promise.

Eddy couldn't stand her. He called us "dorks" and "babies." Called me that mostly. I'd try to think of something to whip back, something about him and his best friend Jack, but me and words don't get along. Every time, I'd blurt out, "SHUT UP!" and then do something that got me sent to my room.

The day I'd led Whitney to Fort Kruse, I'd been so excited to show her something from *my* life. Something as awesome as her house, pool, or pony. I bragged the whole hike in about how my family had built it. About how Dad had designed it. About how Eddy and I had painted the boards before Dad nailed them down. About how Mom had sewed the flag with the *K* that fluttered from a pole on its side. About how we'd made the handprints on its underneath last thing. And while our hands were still wet with paint, Dad had announced, "I christen thee Fort Kruse!" I'd blabbed and blabbed till we climbed into the fort.

Then Whitney sat on a stump chair, pressing her hands between her legs. After a long look at my drawings on the walls, her eyes snagged on our family photo on the shelf with our painted hands held high. "So that's your dad?" she asked.

"Yep!"

Her eyes crept back to my drawings. Frowning at the WELCOME HOME! one, she said, "What are *those* for?"

"For when he comes home, of course."

"Home? You mean *here*?"

The way she said it made me notice that the hammock hung higher on one end, that the plastic table had loads of scratches, and that the shutters squeaked in the breeze.

"Rill...my parents said there was a memor—"

"He wasn't there."

She gave me a sorry look. "Rill, he's—"

"No!"

"Rill—"

"SHUT UP!"

She froze. Then, with a sniff, she said, "You're really good at drawing, and this fort is cool, but I just remembered I need to go." She gave me the biggest I-feel-sorry-for-you smile ever.

"GET OUTTA HERE!" I shouted.

Her hands came up like she was being arrested, except in a way that made me feel like *I'd* done something wrong. Then she took her sweet time climbing down the ladder. I stormed to the doorway. All casual, ignoring me, she strolled along the trail for home.

I fumed around the fort, trapped in there with her words. Kicking the stump chair she'd sat on about killed my toe, but it clunked over and rolled against the wall.

That's when Whitney became my ex-friend. That's when I stopped going to Fort Kruse. And then, a month or so into school, I felt even dumber about the things I'd said that day because all that *popular* and *liking* stuff started.

Now the whole world was having an awesome time while I was chasing my crazy cat up this sorry old trail to that stupid fort. I was stuck in the worst summer of my life!

Checking that Joyce couldn't see me, I yanked off the whistle and threw it as far as I could. I felt a little sick about what Dad might say and almost went to find it. Then, growling at myself, I hiked on up the trail.

6

Now as I walked through a grass-and-wildflower carpet, I kept seeing that girl's hands up as she backed away. What would she do if I even found her? Would she hold up her hands again? Would she sprint away? Maybe she'd threaten me the way I'd threatened her. I paused and moved my slingshot to the top of my pack. Uphill, branches cracked the way they do when something big pushes through. I spied two deer with scared brown eyes. Just like the girl's eyes. How long had she been alone in these woods? I tried to remember if I'd seen her in school last week. Or on Friday, Field Day. An ashamed part of me knew that even if she'd been there, I wouldn't have noticed her.

Clifford zoomed ahead, chasing a squirrel up a tree. The squirrel was way faster, so that cat stopped on a low branch, licking his front paw like *I planned to do this the whole time*. The squirrel scolded him from above. A jay squawked, insulted by the ruckus, and glided to a calmer tree. As I watched its streak of blue, my eyes snagged on white.

The girl sat hugging her shins. Her forehead was pressed against her knees and her hair hung in a curtain, hiding her face. The sleeve of her T-shirt had a little rip in it.

Part of me wanted to hightail it home the way Clifford had shot from the hammock. Sliding my pack off to get out my slingshot, I noticed she was shaking, probably from crying. Swallowing hard, I moved closer, then called, "Hiya!"

She darted behind a tree. Around its narrow trunk, I could still see her shoulder and one elbow.

"You forgot your sack of stuff." I unzipped my pack, nudged aside my slingshot, and tugged out the other *Los*

T-shirt. I held it up with hands that weighed a ton because, man, I was so nervous.

At first she didn't seem to hear me, but then her arm moved like it wiped wet off her cheeks. She stepped out, drying her palm on her jeans.

"Here." I knelt down, lifted out the sack, and set it on the ground, as far away as I could reach.

Crouching low, she grabbed it, watching me all the while with those scared-deer eyes. Clifford trotted up to rub against her hip.

"That's my nutty cat," I said.

She hugged the sack, watching as I shifted onto my butt, facing downhill. I tried to act like I met runaway girls hiding in my fort every day. But I'd never been looked at this way. It made me feel like one of the dangerous things on the mountain.

"I wanted a dog." I tried to shove how uncomfortable I was from my voice. "But my mom said a dog wasn't practical. So she got me a kitten." She'd brought Clifford home last fall, after I'd stopped being friends with Whitney. *Something blue to drive away your blue mood*, she'd said. Now I said, "He's some fancy breed, called a Russian Blue. He's cute and all, but what I really wanted was a red puppy I could name Clifford. You know, like the kid books with the big red dog?"

The girl's eyes were a thousand pounds pressing down.

"But I ended up with a *blue cat*. Clifford's pretty cool, though. He'll fetch, and he comes when he's called—" I re-membered how he hadn't come, how he'd made me rescue him, how he'd made me follow him to Fort Kruse in the first place. "Usually."

He hopped into my lap, nudging his head under my hand.

The girl shifted so she sat facing downhill too.

"Are you hungry? I sure am!" I pulled out the foil-wrapped sandwich, chips, grapes, and bottles of water. "Here." I leaned over and set out one bottle. "Hydration is key!" I opened the foil on the sandwich. It was made from french bread and cut in half. Taking one half, I wrapped the other back up. "No way can I eat all this." I set it beside the bottle of water, then made a show of eating that sandwich, even though turkey wasn't my favorite. The girl watched me from the corner of her eye.

"I can't eat this either." I set the chips and grapes beside the sandwich half and the water. Around us grasshoppers clacked and bees zoomed from blossom to blossom.

There was something I wanted to say. If I'm being honest, it scared me more than when I'd spotted that hammock moving. Words are the second scariest thing in the world, especially if they mean something important.

"I'm sorry," I forced out. "For what happened in the fort. It's a special place, see? I was just remembering that. My dad might come back there, and...well...you can stay. In our fort. If you want."

It was my turn to peek at the girl from the corner of *my* eye. She was watching me with her lips pressed. After a while she looked down the mountain again.

We sat there, with the not looking and the not talking, but definitely not in silence, because what I'd said was loud between us. Also, Clifford moved into her lap and purred. And, of course, there was that pesky creek.

I wanted to ask her name, ask why she was there, but it didn't seem right. Like it might make her sprint off again.

Finally I stood, wiping forest bits off my butt. "Okay, well," I squeezed my pack on, "seeya later."

The girl's eyes shot to me, begging, *Don't tell anybody!*

I nodded once, then started for home. Clifford zoomed ahead, but I had to force myself not to glance back.

When I came to the spot where I'd thrown the whistle, I started searching for it. After forever I spotted a silver flash in the dead needles under a spruce tree. I hung it back around my neck, wondering how different this day might've turned out if I'd been wearing it. Probably with me sprinting away from Fort Kruse, blowing on it with everything I had. I imagined its sound bouncing off the trees and Joyce—all fierce—marching toward me. If that'd happened, I never would've realized the scary thing in the hammock was just a girl from my own grade.

7

On the way back from Fort Kruse, I stopped at the creek and had a stare-off with that loud water. I hated that creek. It churned not just the air but the whole day, even all the days behind and in front of me. Clifford pounced on a grasshopper. I wished I could pounce on that creek and make it *shut up*. Right then, though, I was starting to wonder if wishes *ever* came true.

Three vans pulling trailers stacked with blue rafts rumbled across the bridge into the dirt parking lot and squeaked to a dusty stop at the front door of Kruse Whitewater Adventures. The breeze sprinkled dust on me, making me rub my tickling nose as guests piled out of the vans and into the lobby.

I let out a sigh that I'd been holding all day. Everyone was home and safe.

Everyone except Dad.

I started across the lot, thinking of that shaking girl with her sack full of stuff. Where was *her* family? Was she running from them? She sure seemed to want to stay hidden.

"Hiya, Rill!" Gus called from the side of a van.

He'd been saying *hiya* to me forever. For most of that forever he'd been our lead guide. Dad always called him his "risk bro" because they were best friends and went on adventures together. But now, while Dad was away, Mom was calling Gus her "guardian angel."

"Whoa!" he said as I got closer. "You look dismal!"

"*Dimsal?* I don't even know what that means!"

"Dis-mal," he corrected. "It means gloomy."

"Whatever," I muttered.

Gus really did look like an angel, though, with his blond hair curled in a halo around his company ball cap. And he always had so much energy that he seemed to glow. He glowed down at me right then. Even so, I wished he'd go back to who he'd been with Dad.

"You know, when I feel the way *you* look, what I need's an adventure," he said. "What you need, Rill, is *your own adventure.*"

"Me?" I snapped. "An adventure?"

"Yep!"

I rolled my eyes.

"Let's talk later." He shut the van door. "Right now I'm fixing a problem." Lately Gus was always "fixing a problem." He hadn't been on an adventure himself—big or little—in forever because he was so busy helping Mom.

I trudged across the lot, then alongside our rafting company's brown building. The guides were backing up their trailers and unhitching them from the vans, preparing to drive the tired guests back to their hotels. The rafts at the bottom of each stack looked the same as all the others, but I understood how trapped they felt. Then I pictured that girl in Fort Kruse again, holding up her hands like she was under arrest.

Strapped to the roof of one van was Mom's yellow kayak that everyone called *Ducky*. She used it to paddle back and forth between the rafts, laughing and talking in her guest voice. Sometimes she'd help rescue a guest who'd tumbled into the water.

What you need, Rill, is your own adventure.

"Right," I muttered. Like that would ever happen. My eleventh birthday was only eighteen days away, and probably—no, for sure—everybody would barely even remember it. Again.

Still, even *I* wasn't in the mood for my birthday.

At the back of the building, I climbed the stairs to the

wide deck that only our family used. Clifford trotted across it and through his little door next to the screen door. Resting my knuckles on my hips, I frowned at the boring old picnic table, plastic chairs, and Mom's porch swing. Plopping onto the swing, I thought about that girl again, how she'd wiped tears from her cheeks.

Clifford strolled out and hopped up next to me, licking his black lips with his pink tongue. Since my feet didn't reach the deck, the swing stopped. I pictured Mom as she'd stood alone at the kitchen counter that morning, concentrating on a printout of the day's guests, munching her bowl of cereal. She wore the usual: a Kruse Whitewater Adventures T-shirt, shorts, and river sandals. Her ponytail was threaded through the back of a company ball cap.

Time was, Dad stood there with her, munching too, except on bacon and eggs she'd made. His hair, faded from winter brown to summer blond, was always messy above his visor, even if he'd just combed it. He'd hook his arm around Mom and they'd plan the day. At night, I'd lie in bed remembering them that way, wishing I could stop time. Wishing he'd come home.

8

When Gus and Tom rode up on their bicycles, I was waiting for sunset to end so I could go to sleep and make tomorrow arrive faster.

"Hiya, Rill!" Gus flashed his grin.

"Happy summer vacation!" Tom said. "Wanna play Parcheesi?"

I shrugged. "Sure."

Gus strolled inside and came back out with the game under his arm. He and Tom settled at the picnic table on the deck and started setting it up. Shadows from the little red, yellow, blue, and green pawns stretched across the board.

The silver in Tom's dark hair and moustache, along with his twinkling eyes, always reminded me of a playful seal I'd seen once at the zoo. He owned a shop that sold bike gear in summer and ski gear in winter. He rode a bicycle practically everywhere, even in snow with icicles hanging from his moustache.

I joined them, even though I didn't want to. This morning Gus had said he'd talk to me later, and he was always good for his word. His halo of hair glowed in the sun beaming over his shoulder.

"Joyce said you went to Fort Kruse today." He dropped two dice into the little yellow cup for rolling them. Clifford jumped onto the picnic bench, nudging his head under Gus's elbow so he'd pet him.

"Uh-huh," I said.

"It's been a while since you've been up there. Is it in okay shape? Maybe I should swing by to see if it needs repairs."

"No!" I said, too fast, because Gus studied me. Nice and

slow, I said, "I mean…it's fine. Honest. In fact, I'm going to have my adventure right there."

He tilted his head. "You've got things figured out then."

"I do."

"No adventure advice?"

"Nope."

"Can I tell you one thing?" He held up a finger.

I rolled my eyes. "I guess."

"The best adventures…true ones…they test you and they teach you about yoursel—"

"*Test? Teach?* Seriously?"

"Not like schoo—"

"I'm sure glad you're going to play, Rill." Tom nudged me. "Gus stinks at 'chase, race and capture.'" That's what the Parcheesi box said: *The Classic Game of Chase, Race & Capture.*

"Hey!" Gus cried, but Tom was right. He and I'd escape the blockades and the other players' pawns threatening to gobble our own back to the beginning just fine. Eddy'd get overwhelmed by the dangers coming at him. Gus would ignore them all and get swamped every game. Dad was the same way.

The last time I'd played Parcheesi was Christmas Eve. Of all the boxes and bows under the branches, mine had been the only present for Dad, and it'd made me so cranky and hollow. Whenever I felt that way, Eddy was sure to start in, so, of course, he started saying stuff that made me shout "SHUT UP!" and throw my cup of dice at him, and I got sent to my room.

Now the sun lit the tips of the trees on the mountain like candles. Shadow coated everything below, including Fort Kruse. What was the girl doing? Was she eating the sandwich? Or maybe the chips? Did she watch us that very minute from The Eagle's View? Had she gone back to the fort at all?

"Hello?" Gus snapped his fingers in front of me. "Rill?"

I flinched. "Huh?"

"Where's Eddy?" Tom said, obviously repeating it.

"At Jack's," I grumbled. "Same as every night." Eddy be-ing gone so much stung, even if I was glad he wasn't there to pick on me.

The screen door clapped behind Mom as she shuffled across the deck, concentrating on some papers she carried.

"Hey, boss!" Gus called. "We need a fourth for Parcheesi."

"Thanks, but I've got to approve these ads for the news-paper."

Of course, I mouthed.

"It's just one game, Shelley," Tom said. "It's more fun with four."

She sat on her porch swing but held it still with her feet. "Do you think we should update our website?"

Gus looked at me with crossed eyes, and I couldn't hold back a smile.

From far off, over the noisy creek, came the yips and yowls of coyotes waking up for the night. Looking up the moun-tain, I remembered the girl as she'd stepped from behind the tree. I glanced at Mom, still staring at her papers. Clifford hopped onto the bench next to me and curled warm against my hip. I glanced at Gus's halo. Tom shook his cup of dice, saying, "High roll goes first." And I realized I'd probably been wishing for dark at the same moment the girl had been wishing for light.

9

In the lobby of Kruse Whitewater Adventures, my fingers—even my toes—were crossed. I watched the vans with their trailers rumble over the bridge, leaving nothing but dust. At the counter Joyce gathered signed waiver forms.

"You look jumpy as a trout on a riverbank!" she said.

That made me picture the girl's sack with its guts spilled out. "I need two lunches today."

"Two? You going to Fort Kruse again?"

Around my neck hung the whistle. Squeezing my shoulders was my backpack, stuffed with a flashlight, borrowed from the kitchen junk drawer—right after Mom and Eddy'd headed downstairs—along with an LED headlamp, batteries, and *Chitty Chitty Bang Bang*.

That book was Dad's favorite, so I kept it with me all the time. I loved remembering the way his voice would rumble over the words as I snuggled against him. Since the day he'd gone, I'd been reading to its last page, then flipping back to page one and starting over because all the while I'd hear him. And I could almost smell him, like a clean shirt warmed in the sun.

Clifford weaved between my legs.

"Where's a fingerling like you going to put all that food?" Joyce said.

"Fingerling" means baby fish. She'd been calling me that forever. When I was little I used to love it. Used to love the way rivers and fins glided through her talking. The guests still loved it. But now I wished she'd stop.

Rolling my eyes, I climbed onto a stool and grabbed two clementines from the glass bowl on the counter. "I'm just hungry."

"About time you started growing!" Her eyes stomped all over my edges, and I tried to hide how I was keeping myself exactly the same as when Dad left. She pointed with her chin toward the garage. "You're old enough to fetch your own lunch now!"

I just stood there.

"Go on!" she said.

Clifford and I crossed the big garage, headed for two refrigerators. One held drinks and one held food. Stopping halfway, I studied the high cupboards, up away from all the wet sand and water that spilled off the rafts. Those cupboards held the camping gear for overnight adventures. The heavy ladders reaching them leaned against the wall to one side. No way could I move one of those ladders by myself.

"Joyce?" I called.

She filled the lobby doorway.

"I need a sleeping bag too."

Her bottom lip pushed out.

"Please?"

10

Fort Kruse looked the same as the day before. Same cheery gold color. Same gray plastic roof. Same sky-blue shutters. Same flag with its *K* snapping on the gusts. Except yesterday, in all the excitement, I'd left those shutters open. Now they were closed.

Before leaving, I'd gone back to my room and grabbed the pillow off one of my beds. As I'd hurried down the stairs, Joyce had said, "You're rushin' as swift as the creek!" She handed me the sleeping bag. "You blow on that whistle if you need anything! I'll be listening! All right?"

"All right."

She patted my shoulder, which she did whenever she was worried or proud. If she smiled when she did it, she was proud. If her lower lip pushed out, she was worried. Just then she did both, which looked pretty hilarious.

"What?" I said.

"Nothing! Have fun!"

Adults, I swear. There's a whole world of stuff inside them that I'll never figure out. Some of it seems like things every grown-up knows. Like it's part of a checklist. Like the ones our PE teacher Ms. V uses on her clipboard to keep track of the tasks we need to pass for her fitness test. Fifty sit-ups: check. Ten push-ups: check. Mile run: check.

Other stuff seems private. Like it belongs only to that one adult, and it reminds me of my closet when I clean my room and cram everything inside till the door barely shuts. Looking up at Joyce, I imagined some of that stuff evaporating as clouds that squeezed out her ears. Maybe that's why Mom, Gus, Joyce, and even Eddy looked so serious. Maybe they were trapped in their own private storms. Feeling sorry for her, I said, "Don't worry."

She gave me a thumbs-up.

Now as I studied Fort Kruse, I felt my own stormy expression and realized I was squeezing the sleeping bag and pillow. Loosening my arms, I sipped from the blue above.

I set things down beside the ladder and Clifford hopped on top. I climbed the ladder and nudged up the trap door, but I couldn't really see anything in the murky light. Starting to lower it open, the rope skidded through my hands and the door banged down.

The girl stood pressed against a wall. Her hair was pulled into a braid, but her eyes were still tangled. She held the stick—the one I'd found—like a batter. Her sack was at her feet.

"Hiya!" I climbed in, backing toward the opposite wall, holding up my hands to show I wasn't going to hurt her. "I'm just gonna open these shutters." Unhooking the clasp, I pushed them wide. Sunlight exploded into the fort. "Mind if I open those ones too?" I pointed to the shutters on the next wall.

She just stood with the stick ready.

Moving to the other shutters, I saw the foil from the sandwich, scrunched into a ball on the table. Beside it was the empty bags from the chips and the grapes. The water bottle was empty too.

"I'm glad you ate," I said. "I thought you might be hungry, so I brought more food."

She just watched me.

There was a ruckus on the ladder, making us both flinch. Blue paws appeared as Clifford clawed his way into the fort.

I dropped my hand from my chest. "Clifford!"

"Meow!" he said like *Get over it!*

The girl's expression softened.

Unzipping my backpack, I pulled out the two sandwiches,

two bags of chips (one barbecue, one sour cream and chive), clementines, and three bottles of water. "These are for when it's dark." I set the flashlight, headlamp, and batteries on the table beside the food. I showed her *Chitty Chitty Bang Bang*. "Do you like to read? I'm awful at it. My letters get all mixed up, but I still read all the time. The words inside me are fine. It's the ones coming in and going out that are the problem. Actually, I'm bad at anything to do with school. Sometimes"—I wasn't sure why, couldn't believe, I was telling her this—"it's embarrassing. Except math. I'm good at math. And art. And PE." I set the book on the table.

"Oh." My hand slapped my forehead. I darted to the trap door and the girl cocked back the stick. I almost said, *Really?* Instead, pretending she wasn't threatening to clobber me, I said, "I'll be right back."

I hurried down the ladder, then stood there, deciding if I even wanted to go back up. Finally, I looped the drawstring for the sleeping bag around my neck and wedged one end of the pillow into the front of my shorts. The sleeping bag was the kind for warm weather, so it was light. Climbing the ladder, I thought if Mom could see me, she'd shake her head. *Not practical,* she'd scold. Joyce would watch me with her bottom lip pushed out. *Dork,* Eddy would say. Gus would smile and nod.

Near the top I yanked out the pillow, tossed it onto the floor, and climbed in. I unthreaded my head from the drawstring and set it on the pillow. "There!"

The stick clunked to the floor as the girl stepped back, but the wall stopped her. She slid down it, barely missing my WELCOME HOME! picture. She hugged her shins, pressing her head on her knees.

Well, *that* was a surprise. No clue what to do, I grabbed the clementines from the table and knelt down beside her. "Want one?"

At first I thought she'd ignore me. Then a miracle

happened: She smiled a little. A sniffly smile, but a smile just the same. She took the orange.

I peeled mine, breathing in its smell. "I love these. Don't you?" Chewing a piece, I said, "My name's Rill."

When she didn't answer, I thought how I'd learned to introduce myself in Spanish with Ms. Márquez, the other fourth-grade teacher. Mr. Rainey was my main teacher, but she'd taught our class *hola* and *amigo* while Mr. Rainey had taught hers about life cycles, the solar system, and weather. The popular kids would roll their eyes, but I liked the games she had us play to practice. Even so, learning stuff with Ms. Márquez always seemed like a task I was forced to do. Spanish: check. Never would I have thought I'd actually *speak it* to somebody for real. "*Me llamo* Rill," I tried.

The girl glanced at me, pressed her lips, and looked down.

I fumbled for something else to say in Spanish. "*¿Halbas español?*"

She smiled a little.

"Oops! I mean, do you speak English? I mean... hmm...*¿Halbas inglés?*"

On a shaky breath, she said, "*Hab-las.*" She wiped her nose with the back of her hand. "My name is Perla."

"Perla? That's a cool name!"

I was dying to ask why she'd run away, but it seemed too soon. Silence stretched around us, all the way to that dumb creek. "I remember seeing you at school," I tried. "You moved to town just before winter break, right?"

She nodded.

"You were in Ms. Márquez's class?"

She nodded.

"Did you like her class? Was it fun?"

She looked at me like I was nuts, so I changed the subject.

"I live right over there." I pointed in the direction of home. "My family built this fort. My dad named it Fort Kruse. Kruse—that's our last name. Those are drawings I made for

him of our family. He's been gone, but he'll be home soon."
I pointed to the pictures on the other walls. "That's me, and
my mom, and my brother, Eddy. Eddy's not named Edward.
He's named for the calm place in a river where the water
curls back on itself. You know, how it gets along the edge of
a log, or a rock. And me, I'm named for where melted snow
or rain—"

For the last year and fourteen days, I'd been careful to
remember only things from around when Dad left, so we
could pick up where we'd left off when he came home. Now
a memory elbowed forward, so clear I could feel myself
standing right there in the stubby bushes and puny flowers
near a mountaintop. I was seven, and Dad was a giant beside
me, looking down, his hair messy. *See that, Rilly-girl?* he'd said.
*That's what you're named for. That's the beginning of a river. That
little channel bubbling down is so strong it can move earth. In time, it
can even move mountains.* I was definitely sitting next to Perla,
yet I could actually feel his hug, breathe his sunny-shirt smell.
I was in two places at once, and it made me so dizzy I shut
my eyes.

Clifford hopped down from watching birds out the window and strode into my lap. As I petted him from his nose
to the tip of his tail, I started feeling normal again. An idea
came to me: "Does *perla* mean a pearl?"

She nodded.

Fort Kruse had to be scraping up my memories. Part of
me wanted to get the heck out of there. Drawing a snaky
river in the fur along Clifford's back, I whispered to Dad, "I
wish we could read together." Since I spent so much time
alone, I'd gotten in the habit of talking to myself without realizing it. But when Perla nodded, I said, "Oh! I didn't mean
to…I wasn't…actually…you don't want *me* to read."

"Yes, please?" Tear tracks were dried on her face. Beside
her was that sack of guts.

I crawled to the table, shame rippling through me. "Here."

I tossed her both bags of chips, a sandwich, and a bottle of water. Sure, I was stalling, but maybe if she was eating she wouldn't notice all my stumbles. At least Tate Willisden, Gino Barelli, and Matt Carter weren't around to laugh at me.

Perla tore open the barbecue chips.

Rubbing my sweaty palms on my shorts, I thought of how Mr. Rainey always read to our class. Moving beside her, but not too close, I held the book so she could see the cover. "This picture is pretty lame. I could draw a better one, but I sorta like it for that very reason. Anyway," I said, pointing to an old-fashioned convertible car, "that's Chitty." I pointed to a man driving the car. "That's Commander Caractacus Pott. He's the dad. This is the mom." I pointed to a lady in old-timey clothes sitting beside him. "They call her Mimsie. Even the kids, instead of Mom. I don't know why. This is Jeremy." I pointed to a boy in the back seat. "And this is Jemima." I pointed to a girl beside him. "They're twins." Everyone in the family—the dad, the mom, the twins—had raised arms and wide grins.

Perla studied the cover, chewing. Her eyes crept to my family photo on the shelf, where our painted hands were lifted and we all smiled.

"Maybe *you* should read instead?"

She shook her head. "Please."

"English is okay?"

She nodded.

Clearing my throat, I opened the book. "I don't always catch my mistakes, so tell me if something doesn't make sense, okay?"

"Okay."

11

"Pass the ketchup."

I shot Eddy a dirty look but passed the bottle. He popped the lid and squirted a stream of red onto his hamburger, then a whorl onto his french fries. I held out my hand to get it back and do the same.

He started to hand me the bottle but faked right. He started to hand it to me again but faked left. I'd always been faster than him, so I knew I could just snatch it, but then we'd end up fighting and I'd get in trouble.

"Mom," I said instead. "Eddy won't give me the ketchup!"

"You're such a baby," he said.

Mom didn't look up from her newspaper, just sighed, "Eddy, give Rill the ketchup."

He handed it over. "You're a grump tonight."

"Yeah, so what?"

"So." He bit off a chunk of his hamburger. "Nobody likes a grump. Why do you keep looking up the mountain anyway?"

"Don't talk with your mouth full," I snapped.

"Did you go to Fort Kruse again today?" Mom said.

"Uh-huh." She knew I'd gone there? Joyce or Gus must've told her.

"Fort Kruse?" Eddy said. "I haven't been up there in ages! Jack and I should—"

"No!"

They both stared at me.

"It's just…" I scrambled for a lie. "It's just…well…I'm doing stuff up there for Dad." It wasn't really even a lie, but it sounded way lonelier than I'd expected. I kept my eyes down. Even so, I saw Mom and Eddy glance at each other. Plus, I'd sounded so lonely that I felt sort of sorry for myself.

"Seriously?" Eddy said.

But Mom said, "Shh!" Eyes on me, she said, "Leave the fort alone, Eddy."

"Oh, all right." He sighed—a total miracle—maybe because Mom was his boss now. "But it doesn't belong to just you."

"Duh," I said.

He made a face and mouthed, *Baby!*

Clifford hopped onto the bench. I fed him a chunk of hamburger. For a while everybody but that cat seemed lonely and quiet.

"The guests were grumps today too," Eddy finally said to Mom.

"Yes, they were." But she wasn't paying attention, really. Because her attention was still on me. Before Perla I would've been glad about that, but now her ignoring me was better.

"They complained that their hotels were a mess. And—"

"And the restaurants had terrible service. I know." She looked at him and I let out my breath.

"Word around town is, two weekends back, the hotels, the restaurants, and then the trailer park got raided by the cops," he said. "They rounded up a bunch of illegals."

I chewed my burger and stared up the mountain, half-listening.

"They're called *undocumented workers,* Eddy," Mom said. "And it was Immigration who took them."

He shrugged. "What does Immigration do with all those caught people, anyway?"

"Ships them back to Mexico, I guess."

I choked on a french fry.

"How?" Eddy asked.

"On a bus, probably, or—"

"What's *Immergration?*" I said.

"*Im*-mi-*gration,* you dork," Eddy said.

"Eddy, please," Mom said. "Let's see…to immigrate is to move to a place."

"I know," I said. "Like to live."

"Duh," Eddy said.

"Eddy!" Mom said. When she wasn't looking, I curled my lip at him. "Immigration, the way I used it," Mom continued, "means a part of the government that controls who comes and goes to America. So no one is here illegally."

"Illegal?"

"Oh, jeez, Rill!" Eddy cried.

"What?" I snapped.

Mom held up her hand the way she did when one of us was about to get in trouble. She seemed stretched thin as a gum bubble about to pop. "Illegal means without the government's permission."

"I know that!" I snapped, slumping down and staring at my plate. "But how can *people* be illegal?"

Eddy laughed. "Seriously? I'll bet you thought illegal meant a sick bird!"

It took me a minute to figure out he meant *ill eagle.* "NO, SIR! SHUT UP!"

"Hey, you two!" Mom said.

"And all this time, when people talked about illegal aliens, I'll bet you thought they were sick birds from outer space!" He was laughing hard now.

"SHUT UP!"

"You're such a dork!"

"Eddy, stop!" Mom said.

I popped the cap on the ketchup and aimed the spout at him. "Ah, you wouldn't!" he said.

"Rill?" Mom warned.

I started to lower the bottle, but then Eddy hooted, "Ill eagle aliens!" and laughed even harder. When I squeezed, the red stream splatted right between his eyes.

12

I love when sunsets streak the sky. Since I'd found Perla, though, they seemed to last forever. I sat on the floor at the edge of my bedroom window. From there I could just see where Fort Kruse hid in the trees.

What was Perla doing? I'd brought *Chitty Chitty Bang Bang* home, so she couldn't be reading. Maybe she was eating the sandwich? Maybe she was snuggled in the sleeping bag? Whatever she was doing, she had to be lonely. But *why* was she alone? Why was she hiding in Fort Kruse?

The yips and yowls of waking coyotes drifted down the mountainside. *The Coyote Choir*, Dad always called it. To me their songs were the loneliest sounds ever.

There was a soft knock at the door and Mom came in. "Time for bed."

I took one last look out the window, hoping she wouldn't notice that the other bed was missing its pillow. It'd been so long since she'd tucked me in that I'd forgotten how nice it felt, even if I was getting old for it.

"I'm glad you've been going to Fort Kruse," she said.

I searched her face to see if she was just saying words. After Dad left, she started doing that a lot. Especially without even looking at me. Right then, though, Mom *was* looking. Again. Really looking.

"How is it being back there?" she asked.

"Good. Your flag's the best part."

"Really, Rilly?" She hadn't said that in so long.

"I'm sorry I squirted Eddy."

She snorted.

"He just makes me so mad!"

"He is certainly an expert at doing that." Leaning forward, she whispered, "It was an excellent shot!"

The coyotes sang, closer to home this time. I decided to ask the thing I'd been wondering about ever since I got sent to my room. "Mom?"

"Yes."

Clifford hopped onto the bed, his purring starting up already. Mom ran her hand down his back.

"If those workers—the ones who got sent back on the bus—if they're illegal, how can they be here in the first place?"

Her eyebrows lifted. "Hmm." She tugged out the rubber band holding her ponytail, and her hair swooped down, hugging her face. "I suppose they sneak in, or they have someone make them false documents. Foreign workers, I think, need something called a green card to work in the United States. Some of them might get fake green cards. Some might work for employers who ignore the rules. Some might work for less pay than American workers."

"So they sneak in here to make less money? That's dumb. Why would they *do* that?"

"Because at home in Mexico, or wherever they might be from, they would make way less money." She slid the band onto her wrist. "Or maybe no money at all because they can't find work. Many of those workers come here so they can send money home to help their families survive."

I pressed my hands on the blanket, watching how my knuckles disappeared. I turned them over and they seemed to wave. "Aren't they afraid?"

"Probably." Mom sighed. "In my opinion those workers are really important to our community. They take the low-paying or back-breaking jobs that nobody else will do. They work hard and they keep our town running."

"Like in the hotels and restaurants."

Mom nodded. "And construction."

I remembered Whitney saying, *Shut up, Alissa!* Her dad owned the fanciest hotel in town. He owned a bunch of fancy hotels. Probably they were staying in one in Hawaii all summer. "If they take the jobs nobody else wants—if they help the town run—why couldn't they just stay? Why wouldn't everybody want them here?"

"Well...it's complicated. Not all of them are good people, I suppose. I hear stories about them sometimes, about how they take advantage of our systems, and I get frustrated. But then I think about what I'd do in the same situation to make a better life for you and Eddy."

"What happens to their kids?"

"I'm sorry?"

"I mean, when Immergration takes the parents and sends them away on a bus, what happens to their kids?"

"Im*mig*ration," Mom said. "I've never thought about that."

"Can they come back?"

"The workers sent away on the buses?"

"Yeah."

"I don't know. I'll bet it's not easy. What I do know is it's a controversial issue, and it's hard to know what's right."

No matter what was right, I hoped Perla was snuggled in the sleeping bag and pillow. That she wasn't too lonely or scared. "But they're people, Mom. People are not things!"

Smiling, she patted my leg. "Yes, Rilly-girl. People are *people*. Even ones with ketchup all over their faces."

13

Two lunches and three waters crowded the table. I'd also brought my drawing pad, my bag of good colored pencils that Dad had given me, and some thumbtacks from the junk drawer in the kitchen. Beside those things was the alarm clock from when I was little. It had a plug and a nightlight, and on the back was a place for batteries, for if the power went out, so I'd put some in (also from the junk drawer). If I were spending the night alone in Fort Kruse, a nightlight would be a comfort. The last thing on the table was Eddy's whistle.

Perla sat on the floor, leaning against the wall. She was dressed in the other pair of jeans and the other *Los* T-shirt, but she wore that same belt. I set *Chitty Chitty Bang Bang* on the floor beside me. We'd just finished a chapter where the Pott family went to the beach for a picnic and Chitty Chitty Bang Bang drove at one hundred miles per hour, zoomed through the sky, and skimmed across the sea. Perla petted her little teddy bear, frowning. I decided to find out what had happened to her family.

"Is that your favorite band?" I began.

She looked at me funny.

"On your shirt?"

"It is the band of Papá."

Now I was getting somewhere. "Your dad's in a band?"

She nodded.

"Why does it say *The Dads Can't*?"

She gave me another funny look, then read her shirt. "*Cantantes.* It means 'sing.'"

"The Dads Sing?"

"The Singing Fathers."

I thought about the stuff Eddy and Mom had talked about at dinner last night. About what Mom had told me in bed. I forced out, "Perla, did your family get taken by Immergration?"

She froze. It took her a minute to say, "Imm*mig*ration."

Shame rippled through me. "Imm-*i*-gration."

She nodded.

"Were your parents caught?"

Her face reminded me of once when I yanked a loose thread in my nightgown and it bunched all the flannel.

"Do you live in the trailer park? Is that where Immigration caught them?"

She hugged her shins. "Mamá and Frida, at work. Papá, at home." She pressed her forehead to her knees.

I moved closer. "Frida? That's your sister?"

She nodded against her knees, then squeaked, "I want to go home."

"To Mexico?"

"To my *family*," she said into her lap. "But I don't know where they are!"

I looked around the fort for anything that might make her feel better and grabbed Eddy's whistle. "Here. Blow on this if you're scared and I'll come help."

She glanced at it, then at me. She shook her head, staring into the air with a faraway look. "I miss the farm."

"A farm? You lived on one?"

"Every morning Pablo and I milked the cows and sold the milk."

"You milked cows?" That sounded gross.

"And we sold the eggs."

I pictured a shed with a row of white hens sitting on nests. "All before school?"

"Yes."

"Jeez! What time did you have to wake up?"

"Five."

"Were there other animals?"

"We also had horses and…hams."

"What about dogs?"

"Yes, dogs. And cats." Perla looked down at Clifford. He'd been sleeping in her lap, but since she'd pulled her knees close, he was squished and annoyed. She set her teddy bear on the floor between us and petted that crazy cat instead. "We grew corn and beans. The land was green. So beautiful. Behind our house was the river. In front was the church. All the children played at the school. It was the only place."

"That sounds awesome. You speak English pretty good. Is that where you learned?"

She shrugged. "A little. Papá, he teach us every day also."

"Why did your family leave to come here?"

"*Abuelo*, he is a farmer. He owns much land."

"Who's that?"

"My grandfather." I remembered Ms. Márquez teaching us that word, but, like I said, I never thought I'd actually *use* it. "Life is hard," Perla said. "We are poor. The government, it is…it makes us sell our food only to it for little money. Then the government sells our food for much money to other people. Frida loves school, but it was far. She had to walk two miles and cross the river. It was dangerous. Also, the books cost much money. So Frida stopped, and she missed school for two years." Perla shrugged. "Papá, he worked here for five months of many years. Mamá did not want him gone. So we came—Papá, Mamá, Frida, me. Pablo and Javier, they stayed."

"Are they your brothers?"

"Yes. It was hard. Pablo, he's my *gemelo*…my…what is the word…my same?" She glanced at *Chitty Chitty Bang Bang* on the table. "I looked at him when I was on the bus. He stood with Abuelo, crying. I cried. I cry for him every day. Papá, Mamá, Frida, me—we worked to bring my brothers."

"You mean Pablo is your twin?"

Nodding, Perla looked at the gray plastic roof, but then she shook her head. "Now I am alone! And it is much money!" She hugged her shins tighter and rocked. Clifford squeezed out, all cranky.

"I don't get it. What costs so much money?"

"The man," Perla moaned into her lap.

"What man?"

"There was a man. We stayed in a house. There were many people. One night he said, 'Tonight we go!' We were afraid. We walked far. The man said, 'Here is water; lift the children!' or 'Here is danger!'" Perla gestured a steep down with both hands. "There were lights from…" She circled her arm overhead.

"Poles?"

She shook her head. "They fly."

"Airplanes?"

"No."

I moved to a stump chair and opened my drawing pad on the table. "Show me."

Perla sat on the other stump chair, opened the pencil bag, and chose a navy blue one. Her drawing was pretty bad, but I got what she meant.

"Oh! A helicopter!" I imagined her slinking through the dark, through a creek, down a ravine, all with searchlights stabbing around her.

"There was a hole," Perla said. "We went in the hole and came out. After, we walked far again. To a van. It took us to a hotel. I saw the streets and the lights of the city, and I thought, *We are safe now!*"

"I don't get it. A hole?" She drew a picture of a tunnel under a fence that reached off the page. "What cost so much money? The hotel?"

She shook her head. "The man. The…*guía*…he cost three thousand dollars for every person."

"Three thousand dollars! Each? Why that's…twelve thousand dollars!"

"Abuelo, he sold a part of the farm to make the money to come here."

I looked down at that teddy bear beside her. The bird on its chest gripped a twisty thing in its claws. A snake, I realized, and the bird was an eagle. Its spread wings reminded me of the eagles on the dollar bills I got for my allowance every week. One dollar for each grade, in return for fetching the mail, keeping my room clean, and helping with the dinner dishes. This Friday I'd start getting five dollars every week.

"So, for your parents and Frida to come back, they need nine thousand dollars? Can your grandpa sell more of the farm?"

Perla shook her head and moaned and put her face in her hands. Tears leaked through her fingers.

"Don't worry," I said. "We'll find them. We'll find your family and bring them back."

14

I sat on my bed by the window, making a list of things I understood about Perla on a piece of notebook paper. Clifford leaned against me, cleaning his back legs with big swipes of his tongue. I hated writing things down, but this was what Dad always did when he faced a problem. He'd make a list, then try to fix the stuff that could be fixed. Tapping the pencil against my leg, I read through it.

1. *Perlas famly is gon*
2. *Immigrashun stoll them*
3. *It cost 3000 dollers for eech persen in her famly to crall throo the hol*
4. *Perla has 8 things that she keeps in a sack*
5. *Perla is afrade of geting cot*
6. *Perla has no plays to go*

Maybe now I was finally starting to understand what Mr. Rainey had been getting at. "There's one lesson I want you to learn above all else this year," he'd said on the very first day of fourth grade. With his gray pants, white shirt, pale blue tie, and jolly face, he'd reminded me of a cartoon whale standing on his tail, and—even though I was sitting at a desk in school—I smiled for the first time in forever.

"It's more important than grammar, fractions, or history. Know what it is?" Turning, he wrote the word on the board, the marker tiny in his huge hand. *Compassion.* He said it all dramatic. "Know what it means?"

We all just stared at him. Especially me, because, well, words?

He wrote a slash between the letters *com* and *passion.*

"What does the prefix *com* mean?" His bushy eyebrows lifted. "Com-pany, com-panion?"

"Together," said Corey McGee, who'd known the answer to *everything* since first grade.

"Yes," Mr. Rainey nodded. "And passion, you all know what that means." Tate Willisden, Gino Barelli, and Matt Carter laughed through their noses. Mr. Rainey held up a warning finger. "There's that kind of passion, yes, but it really means feeling. Compassion means a feeling of worry or pity for the suffering or misfortune of someone else."

"People are not things!" he said on that first day, on the last day, and on all the days in between.

A Compassion Box sat on the corner of Mr. Rainey's desk, and we dropped in little squares of paper reporting kind acts from our classmates. Every Friday he fished out one square, and the person whose name was on it won a prize. We kept Compassion Journals. We even had to write an essay about a compassionate thing we'd done. I did the assignments and all, but I never once dropped a name into that box. And never once was my name drawn out. Whitney's was, eight times. Which made me wonder about compassion a lot. I understood the part about doing nice stuff, but I was pretty sure there was more to it.

Through the window drifted the rumble of vans crossing the bridge, back from driving the guests to their hotels. I hopped off my bed.

"Come on, Clifford. Let's talk to Gus."

I hustled down the metal stairs, alongside the building, and into the dirt lot. At the open door of one van, I spotted his shorts, legs, and river sandals. "Hiya!"

Gus popped out. "Hiya, Rill!" He reached back in, lifting out one of the little coolers from between the front seats. On top of the cooler rested his clipboard with the list of the day's guests. "What's up?"

"Do you know about illegals?" I asked.

He gave me a funny look. "*Illegal workers*, you mean?"

"Yeah, those."

"A little. What about them?" He headed across the lot toward the garage, so I hustled to catch up.

"Well, when Immigration catches them, where do they go? Like if they're Mexican?"

His eyebrows lifted and he glanced at me. "Don't know."

"Do they get sent back to wherever they lived before?"

He frowned. "Not sure. Probably they get dumped off just over the border. In Juárez, or another city."

"So they'd have to get home after that?"

He shrugged. "Guess so."

In the garage Mom and Eddy were rinsing wetsuits in the big sinks. Gus set the cooler down in front of the refrigerators. One of the new guides, Mike, set his empty cooler on the counter beside the refrigerators, where they were stored for the night. "Hi, Rill," he said.

I waved to him but kept my eyes on Gus. "Is Mexico big? Would it take a long time to get from *War*—that city—to where they lived before?"

Gus chuckled. "Juar-ez," he said, real slow. "Sure. Mexico's plenty big."

"As big as America?"

"No. I'd guess it's maybe a quarter the size." He set leftover drinks on the refrigerator shelf. "Why don't you check out a map?" Gus always studied maps for his adventures, or when Kruse Whitewater Adventures planned a new trip, or—

A memory elbowed forward. I tried to fight it, but there it was: me, looking across a map spread out on the dining table while I chewed my cereal. Gus and Dad stood on the map's other side, leaning over it. It was Monday morning. The one before I left for third grade, and they left to go kayaking, and Dad never came home. My guts swayed so hard I had to steady myself against the counter.

"What's with all the questions about Mexico?" He studied me.

"Nothing. I heard a story is all, so I was wondering."

"Must've been some story."

"It was."

"Know something cool? Our creek out front, it flows into the Colorado River, right? You've rafted that spot. The confluence. Remember?"

I did *not* want to remember anything else. Even so, I felt the raft bouncing through that churning confluence, Dad sitting tall behind me. His deep voice rumbled a corny joke, and I peeked over my shoulder to see Gus chuckling as he steered at the back. Eddy sat beside me, Mom beside Dad. We all held an oar and grinned. As we came to a calm stretch, an eagle soared overhead. Dad smiled up at it. In that moment I could *feel* how much I loved the river clear into my bones.

That was then.

"Well, the Colorado flows all the way down to Mexico," Gus said.

It took me a second to actually hear his words, but they snapped me right back. "For real?"

"Yeah. It crosses a tiny bit of Mexico," he held up his thumb and first finger about an inch apart, "before ending in the Gulf of California. The Pacific Ocean, basically. Aren't rivers cool?"

No, rivers were definitely *not* cool.

From the lobby Joyce called, "Hey, Rill, I need the mail!"

15

The mailbox was out next to the highway, attached to one of the posts holding the big Kruse Whitewater Adventures sign. Moseying onto the bridge—the two letters Joyce wanted me to leave for the mailman tucked under my arm—I paused to look down.

This water started as a dribble of melting snow down a mountain: a rill. That rill met other water, then trickled to a ravine with a brook. That brook bubbled into a valley that fed a narrow stream. That stream spilled into this wide creek. And this creek gushed into the big, greedy Colorado.

That river, the Colorado, flows all the way down to Mexico.

This water, right here, would flow mile after mile, into a whole other country.

Clifford meowed, all cranky. We usually hurried across the bridge.

"Rill, stop moseying!" Joyce called from the lobby.

As I hustled along, that crazy cat hunted a butterfly into the flowers and sagebrush along the road's edge.

The mailbox's big door creaked when I pulled it open. Letters covered the bottom. Tall ones leaned against the sides. I looked down the two-lane highway in the direction the creek flowed. How far did those yellow dashes keep going? Did they stretch as far as the Colorado River? I pictured Dad trudging along this very pavement. It seemed so far. I imagined my heart reaching out to his, imagined him feeling how much I missed him.

Perla had probably traveled even farther to end up in Fort Kruse. Which meant her dad was even farther away, and if he came back, then Dad could too. My fingers tingled with hope.

Town was about a mile upriver. Looking in that direction, I made out a dirt road branching off the highway. It led to the big white stables and arena where Sir Charles's Shanty lived. Did Sir Charles miss Whitney? Or was she already fading to just a memory? How long till he forgot her? The wind kicked up a whorl of dust on that road. My fingers tingled with guilt.

I stood there, looking one direction, then the other. After a bit I gathered the mail, put Joyce's letters in the box, and lifted the little red flag for alerting the mailman.

Crossing the bridge, I stopped again, this time to give that water a dirty look. I swear, it laughed at me, which made me wobble. I landed against the bridge on one knee, spilling a couple letters. I snatched them up before the breeze could grab them.

"Rill!"

I jogged over and handed Joyce the mail.

She eyed me sidelong. "What's up with you today?"

I shrugged. "Thinking, is all."

She flicked through the letters, squinting to read each one. An idea came to me: "Can I have an envelope?"

16

The next morning Perla sat on a stump chair at the table in Fort Kruse, writing on a sheet of notebook paper with a pencil. The envelope Joyce gave me was beside the paper. Clearing her throat, Perla read what she'd written, except she read it in English.

Dear Papá, Mamá, Frida, Pablo, Javier, and Abuelo,

I pray you are home and safe. I pray you get this letter. I have a friend. She is hiding me in her fort. I am scared to return to our house. My friend brought me a bag for sleeping and a pillow. She brought me food. She reads to me of a family who has a car that flies. I wish we had a car like that. I am okay, but I don't know what to do! Should I go to the church? Should I get caught and come home to you? Where are you? I miss you! I am scared! Please write and tell me what to do!

"I should write more?" she asked.

Her letter was sad, but when she'd read, "I have a friend," I felt proud. "When your parents write back, they'll need a place to send *their* letter."

She frowned.

"They'll write! I know it! Have them send their letter here. Tell them to address it to me. I fetch the mail every day, so I'll just grab it before I give the mail to Joyce."

"Okay." But I could tell it was hard for her to believe me.

I told her the spelling of my name and the address for Kruse Whitewater Adventures. Then I checked what she'd written to make sure I hadn't jumbled the letters.

She finished with *Besos y abrazos, Perla.*

Ms. Márquez had taught our class both those words. *Besos* meant "kisses." *Abrazos* meant "hugs." You should've heard Tate Willisden, Gino Barelli, and Matt Carter laughing through their noses about *that*. With a colored pencil, Perla drew a red heart. With a green pencil, she drew a little line rising off its side. She drew another heart with a line rising off its side and connected them at the tops with a little blue curve like a smile. Humming, she drew three more sets of hearts connected by curves. Music notes, I realized. Then she sang in a clear pretty voice,

Ay, ay, ay, ay,
Canta y no llores,
Porque cantando se alegran,
cielito lindo, los corazones.

"That's beautiful!" I said.

She blushed. "It is called 'Cielito Lindo.' All Mexicans know it."

"What does it mean?"

She became thoughtful. *"Ay, ay, ay, ay,"* she began, "is just sounds. Then it says:

Sing and do not cry,
Because in singing it…makes happy,
My little…love, the heart."

"Did your dad sing it with his band?"

"Yes. And he sang it to me, every day." She frowned.

"Perla," I said. "I'll put this letter with the rest of the mail going out. Just as soon as you address it. We'll find your parents. We'll get them back."

She folded the paper into thirds, slipped it into the envelope, and sealed it. On the outside she wrote *Fernando Infante, Domicilio Conocido, San Sorbo, Zacatecas 99270.*

"Fernando Infante—that's your dad?"

"Yes."

"Perla Infante," I held out my hand to her, "pleased to meet you."

She shook my hand. Then she leaned across the table and pressed her cheek to mine in an air kiss. "That," she said, "is how ladies say hello in Mexico."

I pictured her saying hello to her mom and Frida that way, except here in America, and I realized I hardly knew anything about where they lived. So I asked.

"Our trailer is blue," Perla sighed. "Very blue. In front is a tree with white flowers. Under the tree is a garden with yellow flowers. In the garden a frog wears a sombrero. Always, I lose the...*llave?*" She pretended to hold something between her thumb and finger and turned it. "For the door."

"The key?"

"Yes." Perla's smile reminded me of the lines she'd made to connect the notes. "So Papá made a key for under the frog."

"We never even *lock* our doors. Where did your dad work?" I asked.

She had to think a minute. "He made the warm for houses."

"Like heaters?"

"Yes."

"Where'd your mom and sister work?"

"A hotel. I don't know the name. Mamá, she cleaned the rooms. Frida, she worked in the restaurant. The hotel is tall with walls of stone. It has an...*oso*...in front." She held up her hands like claws and showed her teeth.

"A bear. I know that hotel. I'd better get going if I'm gonna put this in today's mail."

I climbed down the ladder, searching for a lie to get stamps from Joyce. Clifford followed, then Perla.

"Well, seeya," I said.

"*Adiós*," Perla said.

After three steps I turned back. "Hey, can I bring you anything else?"

She looked confused.

"Like clothes. I could loan you some."

"Oh yes!" she said. "More clothes, please!"

"Okay. Seeya."

"*Adiós.*"

From the corner of my eye, I saw Perla wipe her cheek. "What's wrong?"

"You do this for me!"

"Well, in your letter you said I was your friend, right?"

She grinned. "Friend, yes."

17

I rushed into the lobby. "Joyce—!"

She stood with her finger pressed to her lips like *shh!* and the phone pressed to her ear. "Kruse Whitewater Adventures! Welcome to adventure!" she said.

I climbed onto a stool. Clifford trotted in and leapt onto the other stool.

Joyce hung up, took one look at me, and said, "Got minnows in your pants or what?"

"Can I have a stamp?"

"You mean *may* I?"

I rolled my eyes. "*May* I?"

"A stamp? What for?"

"A letter."

"Is that what the envelope was for?"

"Uh-huh."

Joyce opened a drawer and pulled out a roll of stamps. "Where's this letter headed?"

"Mexico."

"*Mexico?* Who do you know in Mexico?"

"A girl." It wasn't actually a lie. "From school."

"I've never heard you talk about a friend from Mexico!"

"I only just met her." Another not-lie.

"I haven't sent anything there in ages! Let's call Mrs. John to find out the postage! Give me the letter, so I can read her the address!" Joyce held out her hand.

Just in time I realized she'd see the writing on the envelope wasn't mine. "Think I'll ride to the post office and ask Mrs. John myself."

"Ride? The Stingray?"

I rolled my eyes. "What else?"

Joyce pointed at me like *No attitude!* "You mean *may* I ride to town?"

"*May* I ride to town?"

She pushed out her bottom lip. "I guess you're grown up enough; I let Eddy go alone in fifth grade!"

That stopped me. I felt torn in half: guilty for growing up without Dad there, but also sort of proud.

"It'll be great to see you on the Stingray! Here!" From a little fridge behind the counter, she got a bottle of water and handed it to me. "Hydration is key! Did you already eat those lunches?"

"Uh-huh." Actually I'd forgotten to eat in all my excitement about the letter.

"Take a snack then. Take one of those!" She pointed to the glass bowl, full of red apples.

I grabbed one and raced up the stairs, through the screen door, and into my bedroom. Grabbing my piggy bank off the shelf, I plopped onto my bed and pried the cork plug from its belly. Clifford batted at the fluttering bills and change that spilled out. I counted ten one-dollar bills, smoothing them flat. Turning one over, I looked at its eagle. Perla's family had spent twelve thousand of these. Just to leave her brothers behind. Just to be illegal. Just to get caught. And now, for even one of Perla's parents to return, it would cost three thousand more.

All of a sudden Perla's dad coming back seemed impossible. *No!* I told myself. *He has to!*

Gritting my teeth, I folded the money and tucked it into the front pocket of my shorts.

৵

It'd been one year and fifteen days since I'd even looked at the Stingray, but now I stood in the far corner of the big garage, staring at it. Time was, I'd fall asleep in bed still feeling

my feet pushing its pedals and my hands gripping its handlebars. Even in winter. The last time I'd ridden it, I'd figured
out how to slam on the brakes so the back wheel would skid
around in a one-eighty. I'd been so excited to show Dad.
Except I never got the chance.

I noticed my whistle hanging from my neck but left it
on to save time. I wiped dust off the banana-shaped seat,
then its curved sparkle-green tube running to the handlebars,
tracing my fingers over the letters spelling its name. The tires
were almost flat, so, getting the pump, I filled them the way
Dad had shown me. I gripped the handlebars, flicked up the
kickstand, and rolled that bike through the garage. Stepping
into the bright sunshine felt like coming near the edge of
something. I blinked at the sky.

"Where's your helmet?" Joyce stood in the lobby doorway.

"I don't know," I moaned.

"No helmet, no Stingray!"

Curling my lip at her, I headed back into the garage, fished
a helmet from the bin of rafting ones, and buckled it on.
When I got back, she said, "Remember the rules! Ride with
the direction of traffic! Stop at every stop sign!"

"I know!"

"Oh, you're plenty smart! It's the lunkers out there that
worry me!" A "lunker" is a big old fish.

"Hold Clifford so he doesn't follow me, okay?"

Joyce grabbed him and he meowed, all cranky.

I swung my leg over and could actually straddle the Stingray without having to lean it to the side. "Seeya, Joyce."

She stayed in that spot, petting Clifford, while I bounced
across the bridge, trying to ignore that ornery water.

18

"Now, let's see that letter." Mrs. John held out her pale wrinkly hand. Her white hair was short and purply. She wore a pantsuit the color of Cheerios and a necklace of green beads that looked like shiny peas. She'd worked at the post office "back to the time of dinosaurs!" Joyce always said.

I fished Perla's letter from my pack and handed it to her.

"Well, I've sent letters to this address before. Another family besides the Infantes lives in San Sorbo. Did you know that *domicilio conocido* is how they say post office? Hmm…" Mrs. John slipped on some reading glasses hanging from her neck and turned the pages of a thick book, peering at the headings at the tops. There was a computer right beside her, but she ignored it. When she found the page she was looking for, she ran her finger down a column and told me how much.

I tugged the dollars out of my shorts pocket, peeled off two bills, and handed them to her. She gave me back three quarters and a dime.

"You have lovely penmanship, Rill. I always appreciate fine penmanship, being in my line of work. It's easier on the eyes."

"Thanks." Looking at Mrs. John was hard because, truly, my penmanship was terrible.

She pressed on a label with the postage. "Is this for a pen pal?"

"Uh-huh. From school."

"Well, isn't that nice! Oh! You need to write MEXICO below the address. In all capital letters." She slid the letter toward me, holding out a pen.

I squeezed on my backpack. "I gotta go, Mrs. John. Will you write it for me?"

She looked at the Stingray leaning against the post office's glass front window. "I see you rode your bicycle, Rill. I seem to remember your father riding that very bike. Am I correct?" She tilted her head and smiled. "And your mother used to ride on the back."

"Uh-huh."

"How old are you now?"

"Almost eleven."

She nodded. "A young lady! You have your mother's lovely chestnut-colored hair. She always wore her hair in pigtails, too, when she was your age. By twelve, your father was already so tall, but you remind me especially of him. You have his sapphire eyes."

My nose tickled at the top. Rubbing it, I made for the door. "Seeya, Mrs. John."

"Say hello to your mother for me."

19

I decided to surprise Perla with her *own* clothes.

The trailer park where she lived was clear on the other side of town, so I rode along, careful to follow the direction of traffic and stop at every stop sign. As I pedaled, I kept glancing at the forest on the mountain. Perla had probably hidden in there the night she'd escaped. With all the fanged, horned, and quilled things. With no whistle. With nobody to rescue her, even if she blew on it.

When I finally got to the trailer park, I stopped and blew out a breath because I looked across about a hundred trailers in there, stretched along a meadow beside the creek. Nothing for it, I rolled down the hill and in.

I pedaled along each street, searching for a really blue trailer that had a tree with white flowers and a tiny garden with yellow flowers out front. A few trailers had yards, but most of them were wedged together, with cars—sometimes lots—parked out front. After growing up in the apartment above Kruse Whitewater Adventures with no neighbors but nature, this place felt too crowded to breathe. It made me jumpy. And for all I knew, Immigration could still be lurking around. If that were true, then I could be in danger. My hands went clammy on the Stingray's grips.

On the last street—the one closest to the creek, of course—I spotted a trailer painted bright blue. A crabapple tree blossomed in its tiny yard. Yellow tulips crammed a garden below it. A bunch had lost their petals, and those stems with no flowers reminded me of ghosts. In those tulips squatted a shin-high statue of a grinning frog wearing a sombrero.

Man, I was so nervous. I glanced over my shoulder but spied nobody watching. Even so, I almost turned around and rode right home. Perla would never know the difference. Except she'd called me a friend. And *I'd* know.

Slinking to the trailer's side, I parked my bike. I crept to the garden and tilted back the frog. A silver key flashed in the sunlight.

20

I made a mental list of the things in Perla's living room:

1. *a green couch with stuffing bulging out of one arm*
2. *a red chair*
3. *a coffee table made from two big suitcases stacked on their sides*
4. *a* Los Padres Cantantes *poster stuck to the wall with thumb-tacks*
5. *a dining table with plastic chairs like on our deck, except the chairs didn't match*
6. *one little table at the couch's arm, lying on its side*
7. *one cup, upside down on the ratty carpet, a little ways from the table*
8. *one brown stain, shaped like a wing, spreading from the cup*
9. *one framed picture of a dad, mom, two daughters, and two sons, also lying on the carpet, not far from the table*

The room's emptiness stole my breath. It reminded me of Perla's sack with its guts spilled out. I stood looking down at the knocked-over table, the cup, and the framed photo. I studied the poster, realizing the man on the right was Perla's dad. I'd had it wrong. He was shorter than the others, but his handsome smile made him seem bigger. I pictured him frowning and bumping the table in his rush to help Perla escape. Why hadn't he run away too? And now he was gone.

I picked up the photo. Brown stuff had dried on it, so I went to the kitchen, wet a paper towel, and cleaned it off. Underneath was a pretty tan church behind the Infante family. I put the photo in my backpack.

A short hall led from the living room to two bedrooms and a bathroom. I went in a bedroom with two twin beds, like my room, except these were just mattresses on the floor.

There was a window but nothing else. One bed was made. One had the covers thrown back. Six tidy piles of pants and shirts were stacked against one wall. Three of the stacks were bigger clothes. Four plastic bins—two on each side of the stacks—held underwear and socks.

In the closet a red dress and a bigger purple dress hung from hangers. To the side hung a pretty white dress that looked Perla-size. Below it shone new black shoes. There were also two pairs of nice brown shoes, one big, one small.

I stuffed two pairs of jeans, two shirts, two pairs of socks, and two pairs of underwear into my backpack. At the closet I slipped in the red dress and the smaller brown shoes. Then I put in the new black shoes. I thought the pretty white dress might cheer Perla up, so I folded it on top, real careful. I squeezed two hangers down the back of the pack and could barely zip it closed. When I tried to slide it on, there was no way, so I had to loosen the straps.

Going in Perla's parents' bedroom made me uncomfortable, so I just peeked in from the doorway. One big mattress was on the floor. More tidy piles of clothes were stacked along the walls. An ironing board stood in a corner with an iron on it. My eyes snagged on a guitar. A spot shaped like a chubby tear was worn in the wood, beside the hole the strings stretched over. That guitar was about the loneliest thing I'd ever seen. Still, I wished I could carry it on the Stingray because I bet it would make Perla happy. No way could I ride with it, though. Not with my backpack so full. And no way could I bounce across the bridge to Kruse Whitewater Adventures holding that guitar. Joyce, Gus, Eddy, or Mom would see it, and that would lead to question after question after question.

I locked the trailer's front door on my way out, feeling so lonely. As I put the key back in its spot under the frog, I started whispering, "They're coming back. They're coming back." Crinkling my nose at the creek, I said, "Dad's coming back too." I flicked up the Stingray's kickstand, shaky all over.

"Hello?"

I flinched, dropping the bike.

"I am sorry," said a lady. "I no mean to scare you."

Was this Immigration? Was I getting caught? No, I decided, because the way her hair curved around her worried face reminded me of a Disney princess at the hardest part of the movie. "You are looking for Perla?"

All my words evaporated.

She glanced at my stuffed backpack. Her eyes seemed to shout, but she said, just above a whisper, "She is still here? Tell her Maria Hernandez says she can stay with her!" A tear dribbled down her cheek, reminding me of the guitar, then of Perla saying, *Sing and do not cry.*

"Tell her Maria Hernandez is alone now also. Perla will know what this means."

21

As I pedaled back through town, thoughts blew through me in gusts that churned my insides.

The little table lying on its side with the spilled coffee cup.

The lonesome guitar.

Sing and do not cry.

Tell her Maria Her—I couldn't remember the rest of the princess's name—*says she can stay with her!*

There was something else too—something way down deep—but my insides were a hurricane, so I couldn't concentrate.

When I came to a statue of a bear standing on its hind legs, I skidded to a stop. I studied its claws and fangs. I looked at that stone building reaching up behind it. I'd been there a ton when Whitney was my friend. We'd sat on fluffy white towels by its pool and eaten popsicles or ice cream. Just looking at that hotel made me super uncomfortable. But right now Perla needed a true friend, which meant being a detective.

Checking the traffic in both directions, I waited for a car and a loud trash truck to pass, then pedaled across the street. I rode along the sidewalk that followed the hotel's front, turned along its side, and parked the Stingray. My insides were a mess, but I copied the proud way Whitney always strode to the front doors of her dad's hotel.

The parking guy recognized me. "Good afternoon!" A big black SUV pulled up. He hustled to it and opened its passenger door.

Ducking inside, I strode past a table with a humongous vase of flowers. The lady working behind the front desk was busy checking in a mom and dad with two squirmy boys.

The boys tore across the fancy lobby and dove onto a leather couch. "Get over here!" the mom scolded as a luggage guy piled their suitcases onto a cart. I turned down a short hallway to the elevators and pressed the *up* button.

I had only one clue about where to find the maids: When I'd stayed in hotels before, they'd moved through the halls, pushing carts full of mini soaps and shampoos, clean glasses, coffee packs, toilet paper, and fresh towels for refilling the rooms.

One of the elevators pinged. The light above its silver doors showed it was stopped at the third floor. The other elevator was at the fourth floor and going up.

"Hurry!" I thought out loud.

The luggage guy got there with his cart full of the family's stuff. He nodded to me. I nodded back.

The silver doors of one elevator opened. I walked in, trying to seem casual. The luggage guy rolled the big cart into the middle and squeezed beside the control buttons. "What floor?" he asked.

I peeked around all those suitcases and saw he'd pressed the fifth-floor button. "Third, please."

The elevator surged up, then made that little sinking motion that I used to love but hated now because it reminded me of the bouncing when I sat in a raft. I was coated in nervous sweat. The elevator pinged. The doors opened. I stepped out.

"Have a great day!" the guy said.

I waved as the doors closed.

If Mom could've seen me just then, she'd have scolded, *This is not practical!* Joyce would've said, *What's a fingerling like you doing in a place like this?* Eddy would've called me a dork or a baby. Gus would've said, *Now, this is an adventure!*

Stepping from the little room with the elevators into the hallway, I looked left, then right. Way down at the end of the hall stood a maid's cart.

22

The hallway stretched long with brown carpet patterned in red and gold diamonds. There weren't any windows, but fake candlelight fixtures on the walls made everything seem dreamy. My steps were silent on the cushy carpet; its color matched the coffee spill in Perla's trailer. My guts felt like they might spill right onto the floor too.

At the cart I peeked into the room. Curtains on tall windows at the opposite end were pushed back, so afternoon sun streamed through.

The brightness reminded me of when I'd rolled the Stingray out of Kruse Whitewater Adventures. Except this time I stood with my toes at that something's very edge. Eyes adjusting, I saw a lady in a gray uniform dress shuffle around the end of a bed. A memory shoved forward: me, lounging on a fluffy white towel, biting into an ice cream bar, sucking the cookie part off my front teeth. There was the dull itchy smell of the pool. A maid rolled a squeaky cart filled with fresh towels between me and the pool. Stopping at a cabinet, she started moving the towels from the cart to its shelves. That maid was the lady in the photo of Perla's family. She was her mom.

The world tilted. I got dizzy. But I stepped into the hotel room, just as this maid unfurled a white sheet high in the air. It floated down to the mattress. She saw me then and startled.

"Hiya!" I waved.

She tried to smile.

"Do you know Mrs. Infante?" My voice was all over the place.

She froze. Her gray-streaked hair was in a low ponytail. Her name tag read Nomra. *Nomra?* I read it again: *Norma.*

I held up my hands the way I had with Perla that second time in Fort Kruse, so she'd feel safe. "I'm Perla Infante's friend." Saying this steadied my legs. "Do you know what happened to her mom? And Frida?"

Norma didn't move, but her eyes swooped all over me.

"Please?" I said. "Perla's scared. And lonely."

Her eyes flew wide. "Perla is still here?"

"Maybe."

She took a long sip of air. Glancing over my head at the doorway, she whispered, "The Immigration came and took many people. It was terrible!"

"What did they do?" I whispered back.

"They took everyone who was not a citizen."

"Why didn't Perla's mom and sister just run away?"

Norma looked at me like Eddy did just before he'd say "baby." She said, "They had guns! And handcuffs!"

"Oh! Where did the van go?"

"The big city."

"The city? Why?"

"They wait in a jail until a bus can be filled. I know. I have done this."

"Did the bus take you to *War*—the city across the border?"

"Juár-*ez*?" Norma whispered.

"That's it."

"Yes."

"Do you think they could be home yet? Could they get a letter?"

"Maybe."

"Why didn't Immigration take you?"

She straightened, rolling back her shoulders. "I became a citizen in the week before."

"You can do that? How?"

"I applied. I had an interview in the city."

That would be awesome for Perla. But first we had to find her family.

"Okay, well, thanks." I started to leave.

"Please," Norma whispered, "tell Perla she can stay with me. Tell her she can stay with Norma Jiménez!"

The hall was dark after the bright hotel room, but I spotted a glowing sign announcing EXIT. Bursting through the door underneath, I almost plopped down on the first step to cry. Squeezing the rail, I said, so loud my voice echoed in the stairwell, "No! He's coming back!" Then I clomped down with thoughts storming through me:

The little table lying on its side with the spilled coffee cup.

The lonesome guitar.

Popsicles and ice cream by the pool as Perla's mom in a gray uniform dress refilled the fluffy white towels.

Handcuffs.

Guns.

Sing and do not cry.

Tell her Maria Her- says she can stay with her!

Tell her she can stay with Norma Jim—I couldn't remember the rest of Norma's name either. I was so dumb!

What you need, Rill, is your own adventure.

Dad! Dad! Dad!

I remembered how, on that first day, I'd decided to keep Perla a secret. How I'd decided she could be my adventure. But *this?* This was way, way more than I'd bargained for. Eddy was right! I was *such* a dork! My heavy backpack thumped like a scolding with each sinking step. I worried my guts might flood right down those stairs and wash me away.

I came out on the hotel's far end, just down from the Stingray, and gripped the handlebars till I felt steady. I flicked up the kickstand and trudged with the bike along the sidewalk toward the hotel's front. A door whooshed shut and my gaze slid up.

"Hiya, Rill!" Gus stood beside a Kruse Whitewater Adventures van, grinning. "Fancy meeting you here!"

"YOU'RE NO ANGEL!" My voice was giant.

"Whoa! You all right?"

"WHY DIDN'T YOU BRING DAD HOME?"

My churning guts finally did spill then, right out my eyes and down my cheeks.

23

Gus stayed for dinner.

"Your mother and I have things to discuss," he'd said. But I knew he stayed to keep an eye on me.

We'd driven home in silence, but when we'd rumbled across the bridge, I'd sniffled and muttered, "I'm sorry I said that stuff."

Gus had *not* grinned. Instead he'd parked the van in the dirt lot and just sat there, staring ahead. His glow was gone and a muscle jumped in his jaw. After a while he said, "Know this, Rill: If I could have brought your father home, I would have. One second he was standing there beside me, telling a corny joke. The next he was lying unconscious in the river at the base of those cliffs. I could *not* get down there. I could *not* save him. Kayaking that section, it was my idea, and it haunts me. Every day." He shook his head. "You're right: I'm no angel."

We sat real still, with what I'd shouted and what he'd just said pressing down on us.

When I couldn't stand it anymore, I said, "He's coming back!"

"Rill—"

I dove out of the van, headed for my bedroom.

Joyce was marching straight for me, her face so fierce it stopped me in my tracks. "I've been as worried as a trout with a hook through its lip!"

"Sorry," I mumbled. And I was. I'd been so worried about Perla that I'd not—for one second—thought about how long I'd been gone. Hadn't even considered that Joyce might be worrying for *me*.

Now Gus sat at the table, watching me, everything we'd said right there in his face. Mom sat beside me, across from Gus. Even though my view of her was from the side, everything he and Joyce had told her was right there in her face too. We ate grilled pork chops and green beans and they talked loud over the creek about business stuff.

Clifford leapt onto the bench. *He* was not worried. He was mad. He smelled of fishy cat food and sat a little ways away, all huffy, cleaning his paws and whiskers.

Perla's parents had to be a hundred times as worried, though. They had no clue if she was even safe. I sipped a satisfied breath at having sent them that letter. At least I'd done *one* thing right.

Taking a bite of my pork chop, I looked toward Fort Kruse. Always when I'd done this before, when I'd wished for dark so the next day would come faster, it had seemed like a game. Now, after seeing Perla's trailer, after visiting that hotel, everything was different. Now I was anxious to visit Perla for her own sake. I had a backpack full of things and a head full of things that might give her hope.

Except I did *not* want to tell her about Maria and Norma. And the not-wanting-to made me ashamed. Because all this? It'd *never* been a game.

This was Perla's life.

"So, Rill, you just wanted to visit Whitney's pool?" Mom said.

This was the lie I'd invented. "Uh-huh."

"Aren't there any other friends you could spend time with?"

I shrugged. After Dad had gone away, I'd just wanted to be alone. Whitney being my friend had been a surprise. And after her I'd wanted to be alone again.

Gus watched me, squinting the way he did when navigating big water with a raft full of guests. I tried to tuck Perla way down deep, where he couldn't see. But if she left Fort

Kruse to go stay with those ladies, or if her dad did come back, would she stop being my friend the way Whitney had? On top of all the hard things I'd learned, on top of what I'd shouted at Gus, this was too much. Shoving my plate forward, I moaned and slumped till my forehead met the table.

"Ah, Rilly." Mom put her arm around me. "Why don't you come to work with us tomorrow?"

"No!" I shot up.

Gus and Mom stared at me.

"No, honest, I'm fine. I'm just tired, is all."

They looked at each other. Probably they thought I'd said that because Dad always insisted we shouldn't start working until eighth grade. That we should just enjoy being kids. But I hadn't even thought of him. I'd been thinking only of Perla. And not thinking of Dad made me feel even guiltier.

Cocking her head, Mom started stacking our dinner plates. The practical way she moved reminded me of Perla's mom in that maid dress refilling the towels at the pool. My insides swayed so hard I grabbed her hand.

"What's that for?" It wasn't her tired voice. It wasn't her guest voice. This voice—like warm honey on buttery toast—I hadn't heard in forever.

I glanced at Gus. "I'm just glad you're both still here."

24

"You're dartin' around early!" Joyce said, setting waiver forms and pens on the lobby counter.

"I'm real sorry. Truly. I promise I won't do that again."

She squinted down at me with her bottom lip pushed out, then nodded. "*Bueno!*"

"I'm gonna grab a couple lunches." Climbing onto a stool, I took two green apples from the glass bowl. Worried that taking two of whatever fruit every day might seem obvious, I grabbed one more.

"All that food, you should be growing before my eyes! Don't forget waters!" Joyce took a swig of her own water.

Mom rushed into the lobby, just as Gus pulled up with the day's guests. He whooshed open the van's side door, grinning as they climbed out.

"Mom," I said, "do we have a map of Mexico?"

She looked at Joyce like *Do we?*

Joyce shook her head.

"I don't think so. Maybe try the library?" Mom kissed the top of my head as guests streamed into the lobby. "Welcome to adventure!"

I crossed the big garage to the counter beside the refrigerators. Clifford followed right on my heels, making sure I didn't disappear again. Eddy was stacking foil-wrapped sandwiches into a box. Stepping around him, I grabbed two.

"What's in your pack, dork?" he said.

I almost spat, "None of your business!" but I remembered Pablo, Perla's twin brother left behind in Mexico. "You know," I said, "I think I get now why you call me a dork. And a baby."

Eddy looked puzzled. His eyes landed on the whistle hanging from my neck.

"You still going to Fort Kruse?"

I shrugged.

"Jack and I will have to swing up there." He waited for me to explode.

"Suit yourself," I said instead. Clifford rubbed against my shins. "Have a good day." I grabbed three bags of chips and started away, but I surprised myself by turning back. I surprised Clifford, too, because that crazy cat trotted right past me.

"Eddy?" I said. "Do you ever wonder why, that day, Dad didn't just stay away from the edge? I mean, it's what he would've told us to do."

His mouth fell open. He didn't say anything, just stood there.

I could not believe I'd asked that, but I tried not to let it show. After a minute I felt like a dork for real, so I said, "Okay, well, seeya." I turned and headed for Fort Kruse.

25

I got to the fort before I even realized it. The whole hike up, I'd been wondering what in the world had made me blurt out those words to Eddy. I was supposed to be helping Perla right then. She was the important thing. And the way he'd looked at me? That was the most embarrassing part.

Fort Kruse's shutters were open. The flag with the *K* hung limp. Perla came to the window and waved.

"Hiya!" I headed for the ladder, thinking, *Tell her! Tell her about Maria and Norma!*

Near the top I eased off my backpack because it was so full I couldn't fit through the door. I handed it to Perla and climbed in. Her *Los* T-shirt reminded me of the poster on the living room wall of her trailer, then the little table lying on its side with the spilled coffee cup, then the lonely guitar.

I knelt down next to my backpack. "I mailed your letter. And I brought you some more clothes." I opened the pack and unfurled the white dress.

Perla's breath caught and she hugged it to her chest. I lifted out the new black shoes. Grinning, she reached for them.

"That dress is special?" I rested my butt on my heels.

"Yes. My godmother, she sent it to me. For my First Communion. Our church, it did not have a priest, so it did not happen in Mexico. I was so happy for it to happen here." Perla's smile unraveled as she ran her finger along a ruffle.

"Here's some other clothes." I pulled out the red dress, brown shoes, pants, shirts, socks, underwear, and hangers. From the bottom of the pack, Perla's family in the framed photo smiled up at me. "And there's this."

She hiccupped and laughed at the same time, hugging the

photo to her chest with the dress and shoes. "You are a good friend!"

Tell her Maria Her- says she can stay with her! Tell her she can stay with Norma Jim-! The words clogged my throat, but I could not force them out. So I told her about what Norma'd said about the guns, the handcuffs, the jail in the city, and the bus to Juárez.

Perla went still.

"I think this is what happened to your dad too."

She glanced at me. "Yes."

I tried again to tell her she could stay with those ladies. Honest. But instead I blurted, "Perla, why would your parents bring you here? Why would they bring you if they knew this could happen? Why would they do something that they *knew* was dangerous?"

At first she looked surprised, then her eyes narrowed. "You know nothing!" She shot up, hugging the stuff from her lap against her. "Nothing!" She took a step back and one black shoe clunked to the floor.

Honestly, I'd surprised myself even more. Still, I said, "Oh, yeah?"

She lifted her chin. "In Mexico, life is hard!" Her eyes flashed. "On my street are bad men. Bad men selling drugs! Frida had a friend. Her father told the police, and the bad men shot *her* to make her father pay for the telling! In the church, our priest, he said this killing was wrong, and they took *him*! No other priest would come. Two years, and still other priests were scared to come. In Mexico, if you raise your voice, you are killed!

"Papá, he went to school three years! Three years! Mamá, four! When Papá came here, he wrote letters to us. He writes like a child!" Perla wiped her cheek, real rough, and another shoe clunked down. "But Papá, he is a good man! He says, 'Perla, if you see a penny on the ground, do not take it. It is not yours!' He says, 'Do not steal! Work hard!' Mamá, she says, 'Work hard in school! Do not get pregnant!'" She squeezed her eyes shut. "In school, my English is bad! Ms. Márquez, she told me I earned the award Excellence in Math, and I did not know the word 'excellence'! I was ashamed to ask her! To our friends, Papá and Mamá asked, 'What does "excellence" mean?' Here is very hard! But here there is hope!" Perla repeated "hope," this time with no voice, then covered her face. All the anger seemed to rush out of her and she folded to her knees, rocking herself and making Coyote Choir noises.

My own anger rushed away too. "Ah, jeez! I'm sorry, Perla." It was the fourth time I'd said sorry. Once to Gus, to Joyce, to Mom, and now to Perla. I was the danged Sorry Fairy, sprinkling it everywhere.

Clifford climbed into her lap, right on top of the photo and the white dress, and he plopped down, purring. After a bit she peeked at that crazy cat through her fingers. Finally, sniffling, she lowered her hands to pet him. For a while there was only the roar of the creek and Clifford's motor.

"I'll hang that up for you." I nudged him off her, set the photo on the floor, and hung both dresses on a nail in the wall.

"I am sorry also." Perla sniffled.

Clifford scratched his ear with his back paw, then gazed at me with his green eyes. They reminded me of a magic green car. That first time Perla had cried in the fort, I'd read to her and it'd helped.

I opened the book to where we'd left off—the chapter where Chitty delivered the Pott family to Paris, then drove them through a mysterious cave with a skeleton, a trip wire, and a stash of dynamite. I loved this part, so I read it, stumbling over words, but I didn't care because Perla didn't seem to mind. I could feel Dad there with me, so I read to where bandits chased the Pott family farther into Paris.

"I wish my family had a magic car," Perla sighed. "At

home we have only the truck or the horses. Or the bus. I miss the horses."

I knew missing horses was just one sliver of being lonely for a bunch of things.

Tell her Maria Her- says she can stay with her! Tell her she can stay with Norma Jim-! I tried again to force out the words, but they would not budge. My danged mouth was blurting out stuff I did *not* want it to—stuff I never expected—but not saying the stuff I *did* want.

I said, "I miss horses too."

And then an idea came to me. A thing that would make Perla less lonesome.

26

As I swiped at spider webs and nudged through bushes, I thought how this trail to the stables I led Perla along was what had led me to Whitney. Eddy and I'd made it last summer. Mom had become practical and was always busy running Kruse Whitewater Adventures, so she didn't visit the fort at all. Eddy and I, though, we went every day.

We'd sneak from the trail down to the creek, to a spot out of sight from home, or over to the stables to watch the horses and lessons. I hated going to the creek, didn't want to see a creek or a river ever again. But I couldn't get enough of watching the stables.

As we got braver, we snuck out of the forest to watch the lessons from the white fences surrounding the pastures. We got even braver and came to the fence around the arena. Or at least Eddy did.

I was chicken, so he'd carry me piggyback to the arena's edge. I was getting too old to be carried that way, but I was so small, and Dad always carried me like that, so we both liked it.

One day at the start of August, a new girl rode out on a shiny black pony. Pink ribbons streamed off her braids as she sailed over the jumps. I thought that girl on that pony was the most amazing thing I'd ever seen. When the pony leapt, it seemed he would soar up and up and up. I was thinking how I'd give anything to have a pony that could lift me to the sky when the girl stopped in front of us. The pony puffed as hard as a train from all the jumping.

"Are you supposed to be here?" she said.

"We're not hurting anything," Eddy said. "Besides, who made you in charge?"

I tugged his arm, so he crouched down, and I held on around his neck as he lifted me piggyback. The pony stepped forward and puffed in my hair. Smiling, I touched his velvety nose.

"This is Sir Charles," Whitney said. "Want to come to my pool?"

"Sure!" Eddy said.

"Not *you*!" Whitney said.

"Come on, Rill." Eddy started away.

I almost didn't say anything. I definitely did not want to go swimming. Even so, I pictured Whitney and Sir Charles soaring up and up and up, and "But I wanna go!" spilled out.

Eddy said, "Fine!" and put me down. "I don't want to hang out with you *babies* anyway!"

That was the day Eddy and I started fighting.

I remembered his surprised face this morning. *Do you ever wonder why, that day, Dad didn't just stay away from the edge? I mean, it's what he would've told us to do.* Why had I asked him that? *Why would they do something that they knew was dangerous?* Why had I asked Perla that? I definitely could not trust my mouth.

Perla and I came to the edge of the forest. I stepped through the white fence around the pasture, but Perla watched from the trees.

"It's okay," I said. "Promise."

She slunk out.

Stepping through a second fence, we came onto the road leading to the big white stables. I strolled along, past the cars parked in the little lot, acting calmer than I felt for Perla's sake. In the arena, Whitney's riding instructor was giving a lesson to a girl on a brown pony. The instructor saw me and waved. I waved back.

"Come on." I led Perla to the rail. The girl reminded me of Whitney when I first saw her. The fences the girl's pony jumped over, probably the same the fences Sir Charles had sailed over, seemed barely anything now. Back then I'd been ten for about a month. In thirteen days I'd turn eleven. Time was flowing along, I was growing up, and I could not stop either one.

Beside me, Perla sighed, happy.

"Come on." I strolled into one stable's long cool hallway between stalls. Its bright opening at the other end reminded me of the long hallway in the hotel yesterday. *Tell her Maria Her- says she can stay with her! Tell her she can stay with Norma Jim-!* I breathed the barn smells—hay, oats, poop, leather—to steady myself and noticed Perla doing the same.

"Does this smell like home?" I asked.

"Home, yes."

"This is Sir Charles." I stood on tiptoes to peek over his stall door. His black tail faced us, but his ears flicked at our voices. He came to the door.

Perla sucked in a breath. "He is beautiful!"

"I know."

"He belongs to you?"

"I wish." I slithered off my pack and fished out an apple, glad I'd taken three from the bowl, and handed it to Perla.

She offered it to Sir Charles as if she'd held out apples for horses every day of her life. Apple bits flew everywhere as he chewed, making us grin at each other. A big piece fell on the ground. Perla picked it up and held it out to me.

"Go ahead," I said, so she fed it to Sir Charles. She ran her hand up his face and under his forelock. "His full name is Sir Charles's Shanty. Whitney said "shanty" means a sailor's song. He's hers."

Perla frowned. Was she remembering that day in the hall, when Alissa said that mean stuff? Maybe coming here wasn't going to cheer her up the way I'd planned. I thought of the pool, wishing I could invite Perla there. Maybe we'd see Norma and the words would come unstuck from my mouth. But Whitney always used an ID card to go through the gate and get towels and snacks. Besides, Perla wouldn't want to be anywhere near where her mom and Frida got caught. Maybe we could go someplace else, though.

Sir Charles nuzzled the top of my head, making me remember Mom kissing me there this morning. *Maybe try the library?* If we went to the library, we could find a map like Gus suggested. And we could see where Perla's parents might've gone. Maybe looking at a map of home would make Perla feel better.

"Hey," I said, "wanna go to the library?"

She frowned.

"Immigration wouldn't be there, would they?"

She kept frowning.

"It's not like they're gonna be checking out books."

Sighing, she scratched Sir Charles in the tunnel between the undersides of his jawbones. It took her a while to say, "Okay."

I thought about the long walk to town and how I'd worried Joyce yesterday. How I'd sprinkled "sorry" all around. Today would be different.

I led Perla out of the stable. "See this road? Follow it until you come to the highway. Wait for me there, and I'll meet you in a little while. Okay?"

She looked worried but nodded.

"It'll be all right. I promise. Here." I gave her my backpack. "Take this. I'll run faster without it."

27

I raced along the trail to Fort Kruse. When I climbed the ladder and lifted the trap door, Clifford trotted over in a huff.

"Had to. You and those barn cats would've fought for sure." I set him on the rung beside me, lowered the door, and hustled down. "Come on!" I called over my shoulder. "I'm in a hurry!"

I raced across the meadow to home, pinged up the stairs, and got my library card from the drawer of my desk.

Joyce wasn't in the lobby. I found her in the big garage, leaning way over a van's engine. She wore her mechanic's coveralls, and the end of a wrench poked from her back pocket. Her bottom lip stuck way out.

"Joyce?"

"Hmm?" Her fingers pinched a wire. As her other hand reached back for the wrench, her Leo tattoo peeked from just below her sleeve, the same height as my eyes, except sideways.

"I'm going…I mean, *may* I ride to the library?"

She glanced at me. "Just the library?"

"And maybe the park?"

"Bueno!"

I shut Clifford in the van. "Let him out later?"

Joyce grunted.

I hustled to the back of the garage, flicked up the Stingray's kickstand, and rolled into bright sunshine. Standing on the pedals, I bounced across the bridge, ignoring the creek. I pedaled fast along the two-lane highway. When I got to the road to the stables, I was all out of breath.

Perla peeked from behind a tree with those scared-deer eyes.

"Hop on!" I patted the Stingray's seat behind me.

She didn't move at first, but then she jogged out with the backpack on.

"You'll have to wear that." I nodded to the pack. "If I do, I'm afraid I'll knock you off. I don't have a helmet for you, but there's pegs."

She looked confused.

"Those." I pointed at little metal posts poking out both sides of the middle of the back wheel. "For your feet."

She swung her leg over and rested her sneakers on them. The Stingray swayed, and she squeaked, grabbing onto my waist.

I'd ridden on the back with Eddy plenty of times, but I'd never been the one pedaling with someone behind *me*. Setting my teeth, I got my foot on one pedal and pushed. The road was flat, so it was easy to start rolling. The balance was wobbly, but once we got going, it felt like sprinting along a tightrope. I whooped. Perla laughed.

By the time we got to town, I was puffing the way Sir Charles had after those jumps, so I was glad the library wasn't far. We passed three streets before I turned right and headed for a brick building with a wide sidewalk and a big glass entrance. I kept our speed up the sidewalk, then braked, and we swayed all over. Yipping, Perla put down her foot, making the Stingray stop like we'd hit a wall. I bumped the handlebars as she hopped off on one leg, like an out-of-control ballerina. We looked at each other with wide eyes. Then our hands came to our stomachs and we bent over laughing.

"That was awesome!" I said between breaths.

"What does 'awesome' mean?"

"You know…amazing."

"Yes." She grinned. "Amazing!" She looked at the library's entrance and her grin faded.

"Come on." Taking her hand, I led her through the glass doors into a hall with a display of art by local people. Her hand felt chilly, especially because mine was hot from riding. When a man strolled out of the library, whistling with books under his arm, Perla's grip went tight.

A danged memory shoved its way forward: Mom's hand squeezing mine as we sat on the wood benches of the town's outdoor theater. People—a bunch I didn't even know—came to the stage and talked about Dad's life like it was over. Like he was never coming back.

"Rill?" Perla said.

Blinking, I started walking again, but then she stopped and pointed at a door with a sign that read WOMEN.

"Sure, okay. I'll wait here." I plopped onto a bench across from the bathrooms. Perla set the backpack beside me. She glanced around, making sure nobody watched, and disappeared inside.

Fidgety, I got up to look at the art. There was pottery in glass cases. Paintings hung on the walls. I stopped at one of a beach at sunset. Palm trees leaned into the front, two seagulls flew across an orange sky, and two people painted as shadows held hands, headed for crashing waves. The seagulls were shaped so weird it was easy to imagine them as flying horses. I studied those shadows on the beach, thinking of Perla and me cracking up a bit ago, of her chilly hand in mine.

Tired of waiting, I went in the bathroom. Perla was leaning over one of the three sinks. Water trickled down her arms, and she was splashing more onto her face. She looked so relieved. Her eyes met mine in the mirror and her expression turned embarrassed. I searched for the right thing to say, a thing I would not have to apologize for later. "I'll bet that feels real good."

She tugged a paper towel from the dispenser. "Amazing!" She dried her face, then her arms. With another towel she dried the puddles around the sink.

I led her across the entry hall and through the library doors.

Libraries are quiet places that I've never been comfortable in. Usually I avoid them. Just then, though, the library's shelves of books, its cushy couches and wide tables, its boxes of tissues on those tables, its hand sanitizer at the front desk, its little kid section with mini-chairs where Mom used to bring me—all of it was a slice of heaven.

"Greetings, Rill," whispered the librarian at the front desk.

"Hiya, Mr. Loven," I whispered back.

I hadn't seen him in forever, but he wore an ironed shirt and tie like always. His beard and button nose made me think that someday, when his hair turned white, he could fill in for Santa Claus.

"Can I help you with anything, girls?"

"This is my friend, Perla," I said.

"Greetings, Perla."

She barely nodded.

"We want to look at a map of Mexico."

"You'll need to go to the reference desk for that. Back there." Mr. Loven smiled, all sly. "You're in for a surprise!"

"Thanks."

I led Perla toward the back of the library, nervous because, honestly, I'd had enough of surprises. Then my breath caught because a whale smiled down from behind the reference desk.

"Well, hello, Rill! And Perla! *Hola!*"

28

"For years I traveled during summer break," Mr. Rainey whispered to my puzzled look, leading us along a low shelf of books. "But last summer Ms. Márquez and I got married, and this summer we're expecting a baby, so we decided to stay put."

Mr. Rainey was married? I'd never thought of him as anything other than my teacher. "Ms. Márquez?" I blurted. "You're married to Ms. Márquez?"

He pressed a shh-finger to his lips, reading the book titles as he moved along. "I am."

"*Felicitaciones*," Perla said.

"*Gracias*, Perla."

Perla was congratulating Mr. Rainey? And he was thanking her back in Spanish?

"Why isn't she called Mrs. Rainey?" I whispered.

He grinned as he kept reading. "She wanted to keep her last name; she's quite proud of her heritage. Now...the atlases should be right in here. Ah, yes." He pulled out a book stored on its side.

"Should I carry this for you?" he said.

Usually I'd have said no, but this was Mr. Rainey, so I led him between shelves to a round table that felt tucked away. He set the atlas there. "Can I help you find anything else?"

"Nah, thanks."

He smiled. "I'm glad to see you two together. Are you having a good first week of summer?"

"Yes," we both said too fast.

He tilted his head, and I knew if we were at school, he'd ask us something else. Something uncomfortable to answer.

Instead he said, "Don't forget to use the index!" Our class had practiced using tables of contents and indexes constantly last year, but I'd totally forgotten about either one.

"Sure thing," I said.

Perla nodded.

"Let me know if you have any questions."

"We will."

He stood there, smiling at us for a minute, then left. When Perla saw my expression, she covered her mouth, giggling.

"They're married?" I whispered.

"One thing of school I know but you do not!" she whispered back.

"Did you know Ms. Márquez was pregnant?"

"Two things!"

"Did you know she was from Mexico?"

"She is from Colombia! Three things! Amazing!"

"Let's check out where your parents might be."

In the index I found the page with places starting with the letter *u*. "Oh, man!" I said at the long rows of teensy print. After inching my finger down three rows, I finally found *United States* in the fourth one. I'd looked at maps before, of course, but never in an atlas. As I turned its tall pages, I saw country after country, city after city, and it sank in how humongous Earth was.

During the school year, when we'd had to memorize the United States map—where each state was, along with its capital—it'd seemed like just a piece of paper. A thing I had to learn for school. Geography: check. Now these maps stood for real places. Places that could separate families. I rubbed my eyes with my knuckles.

Perla leaned over, pressing her finger on the dot for our town. I imagined her pushing on the library's roof, a giant hand from the sky. All of a sudden everything seemed super heavy, making me rub my eyes again.

"Were your parents sent to Juárez?"

Perla pressed her other finger on a dot practically on the fat black line of the United States border at the bottom of Texas. Using my stretched hand the way Dad always did, I measured the space between her fingers. It reached from my thumb to my pinkie.

"Is it far for your family to get home? Once they get off the bus in Mexico, I mean?"

Perla turned to the *M*s in the index. She found the page number for Mexico in a snap and turned to it. She pointed to a spot near the map's center: San Sorbo. I measured the distance from Juárez to San Sorbo with my stretched hand again. It took one and a half. Together the stretches across the United States and Mexico seemed so far.

Perla squeaked and slouched back.

"We'll find them." My chipper voice was miles from how I actually felt.

Turning the pages back to the United States, I found our town again. Then the Colorado River. I traced its twisty blue line through Lake Powell, the Grand Canyon, and Lake Mead, until it emptied into the Gulf of California. That river flowed through Colorado, then Utah, then Nevada, then along the border between California and Arizona, and then finally into Mexico. It was way, way farther than my hand could stretch. I slumped back against my chair.

I'd believed—*needed to believe*—Dad was trying to get home. The same way Perla's dad was trying to get back. But that river's blue line was so long. And I'd waited so long.

A terrible picture formed in my head. I tried to shove it away, but it wouldn't budge, and all I could see was Dad on his back in churning water at the bottom of a canyon. His eyes were shut as Gus shouted down in a panic.

My heart banged. I worried I might puke my insides onto the floor. The top of my nose tickled, so I rubbed it, then my eyes, till the nausea and that picture finally went away.

29

I flicked up the Stingray's kickstand, but we didn't climb on. Instead Perla and I moseyed along, the backpack hanging from one of my shoulders. We didn't talk, just stared at the sidewalk, concentrating on private stuff.

Do you ever wonder why, that day, Dad didn't just stay away from the edge? I mean, it's what he would've told us to do. Such a weird thing to ask Eddy. *Why would they do something that they knew was dangerous?* Such a weird thing to ask Perla. As we walked along, I squeezed the Stingray's handlebars because those questions dribbled down my raw insides.

We went into the park beside the library and sat on the lawn at the edge of a pond. I opened my backpack and fished out our lunch: egg salad sandwiches, my favorite. From how Perla gobbled down hers, she must've loved them too.

Ducks paddled around and quacked and fought, making a ruckus. One duck got mad and flapped away, splashing us. I thought of Perla's relieved expression when she'd washed herself in the bathroom. *Tell her Maria Her- says she can stay with her! Tell her she can stay with Norma Jim-!* If Perla stayed with one of those ladies, she could have an actual shower. If she stayed with one of them, she could eat something besides sandwiches and potato chips.

Right that minute I tried to tell her about them. Truly. But that twisty blue line came rushing back. And then came that horrible picture of Dad in that river with Gus shouting down. This time I felt sick clear to my fingers and toes. I wrapped my sandwich back up, shaky all over.

We headed for the playground. Perla wandered over to one of the swings, so I set the Stingray and my backpack down, then plopped onto the one beside her. Pretty soon we were soaring as high as the chains could go.

The wind against my face felt clean and good. Shutting my eyes, I leaned back as I swooped forward. There came that second between up and down, then the falling, falling, before the chains jolted. Had Dad felt that same falling? Except chains never stopped him.

The clouds had coated the sky, and now *they* seemed like the sky and the patch of blue seemed a cloud. Everything was inside out.

"I love to swing!" Perla shouted. "I wish I could fly!"

My voice felt so far away that it took me a second to shout back. "Then you'd never fall!"

"Then I could fly to my family!"

"Or they could fly back to you!"

"Like Chitty!"

"You two are losers!" Tate Willisden leaned against a swing set post, smirking. Gino Barelli and Matt Carter stood behind him. Tate was only a little taller than me, but Gino and Matt were way taller. For some reason they did whatever Tate commanded, even though it usually meant trouble. Which was weird because Tate's dad was the sheriff.

"Mind your own business!" I shouted and kept swinging. But Perla started dragging her sneakers through the gravel.

"Why are you hanging out with *her*?" Tate said. Last year he and Whitney had actually been boyfriend and girlfriend.

"Go away!" I spat.

Perla was slowing down, so I dragged my sneakers too, making a puff of dust each time I passed.

"Does she even speak English? I mean, I know you're not popular, but what are you? Desperate?"

Gino and Matt laughed through their noses.

Perla stopped, staring at her feet.

My swing was at the same level as Tate's narrowed eyes. I narrowed my eyes right back and growled, "Shut up!"

He could be the meanest laugher you ever saw, and he laughed that way now. Gino and Matt joined him. He stepped away from the post, just beyond where I was. "I can't believe you're friends with a Mexican!" Turning, he gestured *Let's go!* to Gino and Matt.

I let go of the chains and flew out of the swing, right into Tate's back. We smashed to the gravel. I was on my knees in a snap, slugging his back. Out the corner of my eye, I could see Gino's and Matt's open mouths.

"TAKE IT BACK!" I shouted.

Tate howled, "Help!"

Gino plowed into me, but I rolled out from under him and onto my feet.

Tate staggered up.

Gino grabbed my arm. I yanked it away, breathing through my teeth. My hands were ready fists. "Didn't you listen to Mr. Rainey?" I snarled.

"Mr. Rainey's an idiot!" Tate said.

Roaring, I charged into him, head first. He landed on his back, all his breath whooshing out. My first lightning-fast punch into his face felt awesome, like I was hitting all of Tate's meanness. The second felt like I was hitting the whole cruel world. The third was mushy, and his nose crunched against my knuckles, and he whimpered.

A silver glint caught my eye: my whistle. I shot off him, wiping my nose with the back of my hand. Even though I was kicking his butt, I was the one gushing tears.

Tate wobbled to his feet. Blood ran down his chin, then his neck, and bloomed against the collar of his white T-shirt. I could tell he wanted to cry. Heaving breaths, I remembered flowers. Flowers everywhere at Dad's memorial service. And tears. Tears on every face there.

Except mine.

Gino and Matt stood behind Tate, staring like I had fangs, horns, or quills.

Perla appeared beside me. Her chin lifted real slow.

"Mr. Rainey is not an idiot!" I growled. "And she's got a name! It's Perla, and she's *my friend*!"

"I'm telling!" Tate said.

"*Telling?* Telling what? That a girl beat you up? GET OUTTA HERE! YOU...YOU...BABY!"

"No! I'm telling that an illegal is in the park! Right now!" He turned to Gino and Matt. "Come on!" he commanded, and they jogged off toward town's center. Toward the sheriff's station.

30

I pedaled the Stingray as fast as my legs would go, breathing hard as a train. Perla held tight to my waist, and I saw her worried expression each time I glanced over my shoulder for the flashing lights of a police car.

Finally the road to the stables came up on our left. Looking both directions, I turned across the highway. As we bounced off the pavement onto dirt, I slumped on the Stingray's seat. All my fury had evaporated and my insides had gone cold and sloshy.

I braked, then Perla hopped around on one leg again, but neither of us laughed now. We trudged, me pushing the Stingray between us. When we came to the stable's bridge over the creek, a car drove toward us. Since the bridge was narrow, we waited for it to pass. Whitney's riding instructor waved from behind the steering wheel. I waved back, trying to look like life was dandy.

We crossed the bridge in the car's dust. My knuckles throbbed. I'd only ever hit Eddy before, and never that way. The willies rushed through me as I remembered the squishy feel of Tate's face.

On the bridge's other side, I set the Stingray down in the grass and flowers, knelt on the edge of the bank, and crinkled my nose at that water. My knuckles were pounding, but my heart went so still I wondered if it beat at all. After forever I dipped my hands into that terrible creek.

Perla knelt beside me.

"Boy, I've made a problem now. I'm sorry."

"No, Rill." She leaned over to see my face. "This boy... Tate...he is mean always at school. He pushes. He takes things…the coats, the lunches. We find them in the snow."

"You should've told someone. Mr. Rainey would've—"

"We do not say anything! We do not want trouble. Our parents ask, 'How is school?' and we say, 'Good!'"

"Seriously?"

Perla shook her head. "What can they do? They can only worry."

I frowned and Perla studied my expression.

"Sometimes, Mr. Rainey or Ms. Márquez, they catch Tate," she said. "And PE—that is the best! Ms. V, she catches Tate always! I love Ms. V!"

"She did?" I said. "You do?"

"Yes!"

I stood, my numb dripping hands like cold red gloves.

Back on the road, we moseyed over to the place where we needed to follow the white fence around the pasture's edge to get on the trail to Fort Kruse.

"I guess we can't go back to town," I muttered. "At least for a while."

Perla nodded.

"Dang it!" What was wrong with me? Now it wasn't just my mouth I couldn't trust; I couldn't trust my fists either.

We came to the fence. No way could I push the Stingray through the grass and sagebrush, and, honestly, I was too worn out to even walk up there. Tired from riding Perla to town. Tired from Mr. Rainey changing. Tired from seeing the far distance to Perla's family. Tired from seeing that river's twisty blue line. Tired from my fight with Tate. Tired from rushing back to this spot. Tired, most of all, from that horrible picture of Dad in that churning river with his eyes shut.

Gus's words from when we'd played Parcheesi—way back when all this started—came to me: *The best adventures…true ones…they test you and they teach you about yourself—*

Maybe I shouldn't have cut him off.

"Okay, well, I'll come to Fort Kruse tomorrow morning."

I glanced at the sun, barely a glow through the clouds. "Hey, look!" I pointed to a rainbow spraying out one side.

"¡*Arco iris!*" Perla cried.

That rainbow whispered hope.

"Well, seeya." I turned the Stingray around and swung one leg over it.

"*Adiós.*"

As I glanced back at the sky, an idea came to me: Perla could stay in the fort but take showers and eat other food. All she had to do was walk out the trail to the stables. Then we'd meet here, ride the Stingray along the highway, and cross the bridge to home. We'd never see Tate or anyone, except Mom, Eddy, Gus, and Joyce. Maybe Tom or Leo. Perla could come every day, visiting like a normal friend. When I rode her back to the stables in the afternoons, we could check the mail for the letter from her parents. And we could visit Sir Charles.

"Perla!" I called.

31

The next morning, after Mom, Gus, and Eddy left, I pedaled with sore legs along the two-lane highway. "Leave Fort Kruse at nine thirty," I'd told Perla yesterday. "I'll leave my house at nine thirty. We should get there about the same time. Meet me at Sir Charles's stall." Perla'd had those deer eyes but nodded.

Now I turned onto the dirt road to the stables, crossed the bridge, and pedaled along the white fences around the pastures. I pedaled past the arena and parked the Stingray. A teenager was pushing a wheelbarrow of poop through the hallway of stalls, but nobody was near Sir Charles. I walked to his gate, peeked over, and said, "Hiya!"

He nickered and arched his neck over the door to nudge me.

"You wanna treat? Okay." I wriggled off my backpack and fished out an apple. My stiff hand wouldn't straighten as I held it out on my palm. Sir Charles stretched his lips around it—which was hilarious—and chomped down. Chunks fell to the dirt. As he chewed, I petted his velvety nose. He nudged me again, wanting the rest of the apple, so I picked up the chunks and fed them to him.

Leaning against the stall door, I petted his neck. "Have you ever been in a fistfight? Nah, I'll bet not. It sure feels weird after."

He chewed and tossed his head, agreeing.

"Do you ever wish you could fly?"

This time he just chewed, real loud.

"Do you miss Whitney? Do you remember her a little less every day?" I rubbed a lock of his mane between my fingers.

"I've been trying so hard to stay exactly like I was when Dad left, but I'm changing anyway. I don't know what to do. Do you think Dad will—?"

Hearing steps, I looked up. Bright sun lit the stable's open doorway, so as Perla walked toward me, she was only shadow. When she got closer, I stepped out from behind Sir Charles. She saw me and smiled with relief.

"*Hola, amiga,*" I said, sort of shy.

"Hiya!" With her accent, it sounded so ridiculous that we busted out laughing.

≪

"Joyce looks scary, but she's nice," I shouted over my shoulder, pedaling the Stingray along the highway with Perla on back. As we got closer to home, I started feeling nervous. Sweaty even. "There's our road."

Perla pointed at our company sign. "This is you!"

It was as big as one of the vans, but I couldn't even look at it. Even so, I knew it announced KRUSE WHITEWATER ADVENTURES across its top in orange letters, and that at its bottom an arrow pointed toward home. I knew, too, that the background was a photo of Dad, Mom, Eddy, and me rafting through rapids with Gus steering at the back.

I turned onto the dirt road, passing the sagebrush and flowers. As we pedaled onto the bridge, I shot the creek a mean look. We rolled across the dirt lot and into the big garage, straight to the back. Perla hopped off, and while I parked the Stingray, she took in the two refrigerators, the countertop next to them, the racks of wetsuits beside the big sinks, the bins of helmets, the stretch of concrete with the drains where they rinsed off the rafts, the high cupboards, and the one van Joyce had been working on yesterday. Its hood was still up.

Clifford trotted over, grumpy because Joyce had kept him from following me. Perla picked him up and nuzzled him.

"Your family, it brings people on the river?" she asked.

I shrugged. "Yeah. In winter they tour people around on snowmobiles."

Perla looked confused.

"You know, a sled with a motor. For the snow. My dad always calls snow 'whitewater.' He's always making corny jokes."

"I don't know this word 'snowmobile,'" Perla said.

"There's a bunch parked on the other side of this building. You can see them from the fort."

She looked confused.

"I'll show you." I led her into the lobby.

Joyce had the phone pressed to her ear and squinted at the computer screen behind the counter. She wore her mechanic's coveralls halfway zipped to her waist. "Got it," she said into the phone. "You're confirmed. Two adults, two minnows, for Thursday." As she typed, Perla stared at her muscles and tattoo.

I climbed onto a stool. Perla climbed onto the stool beside me, all nervous. I handed her a winter brochure from a stack on the counter. "Those are snowmobiles." On it Gus was driving one, dressed in his guide coat and pants. Behind him Dad drove another snowmobile with me in front. Mom drove one with Eddy sitting behind her. It was the winter of third grade. The rafting photo on our sign by the highway had been taken in the spring that followed, as we'd rafted the confluence, the week before Dad left.

"This is you also!" Perla said.

"Uh-huh."

Joyce hung up the phone and looked at us. "Well, hello!"

"This is Perla," I said.

Joyce's bottom lip pushed out. Then she leaned across the counter, "¡Con gusto!" She pressed her cheek to Perla's, giving her an air kiss.

I blurted, "You knew about that kissing-hello thing?"

"Of course!" She took a swig of water. At my surprised

expression, she said, "You want me to say hello to *you* that way?"

"Maybe."

"*Bueno!*" Leaning across the counter, she pressed her cheek to mine and gave me an air kiss. She said to Perla, "You might be a good influence!"

Perla looked confused.

Joyce repeated what she'd said in Spanish.

Perla smiled but looked embarrassed.

Joyce talked to her some more. If she talked slowly, I could understand some of the things she said, but now she talked fast.

Perla answered in Spanish. Fast.

Joyce asked something else. Fast.

Perla looked at me, considering, then she gave a long answer. I couldn't believe how she talked because until that moment she'd spoken only careful English, sort of slow. Now Spanish flowed out of her in long musical sentences.

Joyce watched Perla close too. She asked something short.

Perla gave another long answer.

Joyce nodded. Her eyes moved to my swollen knuckles. She asked another short question and Perla answered.

I slumped to my elbows on the counter. Was Perla telling Joyce about her family being caught? Was she telling her about my fight with Tate? I thought I heard her say, "Sir Charles."

Joyce glanced at me in a thinking way.

"What are you talking about?" I blurted.

"Perla is telling me how much you two love that over-priced pony of Whitney's! Why didn't you tell me you'd been going to the stables?"

I shrugged.

Joyce frowned. "Perla, see if you can get your mom to drive this last bit and drop you off here! If not, I can drive over there in a vehicle and get you!"

What had she told Joyce?

Perla's gaze hopped from Joyce to me. She seemed desperate but trying not to show it, so I said, "I...I wanna ride the Stingray over." Not a lie, really. "I promised Whitney I'd keep Sir Charles from getting lonesome anyway."

"And why would you do that for *her*?"

"Ah, she's not so bad." With a snort, I realized that wasn't a lie either.

"Hmm." Joyce took another swig of water, giving me a thinking look. "All right."

Leo strolled into the lobby, wearing coveralls that matched Joyce's.

"Hiya, Leo," I said.

Joyce pulled her coveralls on all the way and zipped them up.

"Hi, Th-rill," he said.

To Perla I said, "'Thrill' means fun and exciting. It's a compliment, I guess."

"Sure is!" Leo said.

Holding out her hand toward Perla, Joyce said something formal-sounding in Spanish that ended with "Perla Infante."

Leo nodded to her and winked.

Perla said something that seemed like *Pleased to meet you.*

Joyce and Leo disappeared into the garage.

"What did you tell her?" I whispered.

Perla made a face. "Joyce is nice, yes, but I was scared! I said Mamá works at the stables."

"Oh! Whew! That was smart!" I grabbed two clementines from the bowl beside me and held one out for her. "Come see my house."

32

As I led Perla past the one trailer stacked with blue rafts that hadn't gone out for the day, I realized I felt the way that raft on top looked, light and floaty because she was with me.

Climbing the stairs, I listened to her sneakers pinging against each metal step. Their sound made my own steps seem less lonely. We came to the wide deck and Clifford strolled onto it, flicking his tail, showing off.

"This is where we hang out most of the time in summer," I said.

Perla looked at the picnic table, plastic chairs, and porch swing. I thought of the plastic chairs in her trailer. Ours were nicer.

I plopped onto the swing. "My mom calls this her deck swing. She says it's not a porch swing because it's not on a porch."

"I do not understand." Perla plopped down beside me. Clifford hopped up between us.

"Maybe...um." What *did* Mom mean when she said that? Porches were nice, but decks were nice too. And this deck had a view up the mountain that could be on a postcard. "Mom calls herself a practical woman."

"What is 'practical'?"

I frowned. "Hmm...not fun? Always working? Hardly ever smiling?"

Perla sighed. "My family works always."

I pictured her mom at the pool, stacking those towels. I pictured Mom, stacking the plates. I felt Mom's hand as I'd squeezed it. Felt Perla's hand in mine at the library. Felt Tate's squishy face against my knuckles. I wrestled back that picture of Dad, eyes shut, in the river. Since our feet didn't touch the ground, the swing stopped.

Perla cocked her head. She unbuckled her belt and tugged it off. Buckling it around one of the swing's legs, she held on to the other long end and pulled. We started swinging.

"Holy cow!" I said. "That's smart!"

"I love to swing." Her smile was sly.

Another memory shoved forward: Mom and me sitting right here. *This isn't a porch swing, it's a deck swing,* she said.

But Dad calls it a porch swing! I said.

Yes, well, he's gone, Rill. We're going to need to buckle down and start accepting things for how they really are.

I felt myself fly off from right where I sat, felt myself churn to face Mom. Felt my fists press my hips. Felt myself shout, *TAKE IT BACK! HE'S COMING HOME! HE IS!* And then I felt myself sprint to my room.

I almost grabbed Perla's hand as a lifeline, but I didn't want to seem like a dork. So we just swung with that creek loud around us. We peeled our clementines and ate them.

"See over there?" I pointed to the mountain. "That's where Fort Kruse is. At night I watch and cross my fingers that you aren't scared."

"I see this place," Perla said. "The lights in night. In day I see it also." She thought for a minute. "At night I am not scared."

"You're not?"

"A little." She shrugged. "But there are things more scary than night."

On my street are bad men.

We go in the hole and come out.

Handcuffs.

Guns.

The little table lying on its side with the spilled coffee cup.

The lonesome guitar.

Dad! Dad! Dad!

"What is your favorite color?" Perla asked.

"Orange. But not this shade." I held up the peels. "I love the color of the inside fruit. It's also the orange of sunset, or on the belly of a trout. Know what I mean?"

"Yes. It is beautiful."

"What's your favorite?"

"Blue. I do not know the word. Blue blue. The blue of the sky with no clouds. At a house where Papá worked, a man bought a paint that was wrong. Papá, he saw the color was my favorite, and he took it home to paint our trailer. To make me happy."

"*He* painted it that color?"

"Yes."

I worried Perla might turn sad, but she just smiled.

"I still can't believe Mr. Rainey is married to Ms. Márquez."

"They married in my church."

"No way!"

"That is four things I know!"

We swung. After a bit she sang in that clear voice:

Ay, ay, ay, ay,
Canta y no llores,
Porque cantando se alegran,
cielito lindo, los corazones.

"That's a good song," I said. "Is there more?"

She sang the whole song. It had a cheery rhythm, and as she sang, my insides calmed.

"The *'ay, ay, ay, ay'* part is awesome," I said.

"You should hear Papá sing it!"

I remembered the lonely guitar, but I'd had enough of remembering. I hopped off the swing. "Let's go inside."

"Living room." I pointed to the couch, TV, coffee table, and two recliners. I pointed to the dining table. "In summer we eat only breakfast there. And this," I strode down the hall, "is my room." I plopped onto my bed by the window.

Perla stood in the doorway, taking in the beds, the nightstand, and the dresser with its mirror. She looked at my desk and the shelves above with my books, photo album, and piggy bank. She walked in real slow and sat on the other bed, seeming worried about mussing it up, which was pretty funny because clothes were all over the floor, and the bed I sat on wasn't even made. I'd have to tidy up before Mom got home if I wanted my allowance. When Perla saw the wall with the door she'd come through, her breath caught. "That is beautiful!"

I shrugged.

She stepped close to that wall, amazed by its mural of a white unicorn flying toward a rainbow. Around it clouds glowed with sunset. Below stretched Kruse Whitewater Adventures with its green roof and brown walls, its vans and trailers with rafts on one side, its snowmobiles on the other. All of this was snuggled along the banks of the creek. Pine trees covered the mountains. A barefoot girl in a nightgown rode the unicorn, chestnut-colored hair streaming down her back.

"This is you!" Perla said.

My guts churned so hard I worried I'd be sick.

"Who painted this?"

I didn't answer. Couldn't answer. So I stood. "Want to use my shower?"

"Perla, this is my mom."

Mom turned from washing wetsuits in the big sinks. She looked worn out but surprised. "Hello, Perla," she said in her guest voice.

"And Eddy," I sighed.

He looked surprised too, but even more tired. He didn't say anything, just stood there across from Perla with his wet hands, and I realized he'd gotten tall.

"Is it okay if we have a sleepover?" I asked.

"Of course. If it's okay with your parents, Perla, we're happy to have you."

"It is okay," Perla said.

"Perfect!" Mom said. "Why don't you call them on the phone in the lobby. Let me dry off, and I'll be there in a minute."

I'd forgot how Mom insisted on talking to parents before a sleepover. And no wonder: I hadn't had one in forever. I headed for the lobby with Perla following.

"Hustle, Rill! I need the mail!" Joyce said.

"Sure thing!" She handed me the letters to go out, and I marched through the lobby door, happy for the chance to think. I slowed to moseying. "What are we gonna tell my mom?"

Perla shrugged. "The truth."

The truth? I'd be in big trouble if Mom, Eddy, Gus, and Joyce knew I'd punched Tate Willisden. But if they found out Perla was stranded with no family and I'd been hiding her, I'd end up in even bigger trouble. And would they call Immigration?

Tell her Maria Her- says she can stay with her! Tell her she can stay with Norma Jim-! Oh, I'd done things all wrong! If I'd told Perla right away about those ladies, then she'd be staying with one of them and Mom would have someone to call.

"We do not have a phone," Perla said.

"What?"

"All our money goes to Mexico. To bring my brothers. The house beside us, we use the phone there."

"Oh!" I started feeling better. "So my mom couldn't call anybody, even if your parents were here?"

Perla nodded. "I will tell her this."

"Joyce might tell her to call the stables."

Perla shrugged. "Mamá works there only until lunch. Now she is at her other work where there is no phone. She said already a sleepover was okay." Halfway across the bridge, Perla stopped to look down at the frothy water. "Amazing!"

Clifford meowed, impatient.

"All this melting snow slows down by the Fourth of July, and the creek gets way smaller. Big water's the best rafting, though, so my family works a ton this time of year. Right now they start a few miles downriver, where the banks are wider. It's too narrow and rough here."

"Your family is brave. This water scares me."

"It scares me too."

"No! How can it scare you?"

"Let's go. Joyce needs the mail."

We got to the mailbox. I opened its big creaky door and checked for a letter from Mexico. There wasn't one.

"It'll come, Perla. We'll keep checking every day. We'll find your parents."

As we walked back, Gus pulled up beside us in a van. "Hiya, Rill!" he called out the open passenger window.

"Hiya, Gus. This is Perla."

"Hiya, Perla!"

She waved.

"Hey, Gus," I said. "Perla's sleeping over. Can you and Tom come play Parcheesi tonight?"

He flashed a grin. "Sure! Tom'll love that! Wanna ride?"

"No thanks. We'll walk," I said, relieved because I'd been worried about what Perla and I would do for the night. Gus drove on, kicking up dust.

"What is Parcheesi?" she asked.

"It's a game. You have these four men, and you race them around the board to home before anyone catches them and sends them back to the start. It's fun."

She glanced at me like I was teasing her.

"I'm serious," I said.

On the bridge she stopped again. This time she pressed her hands on her legs so she could lean farther out over the edge.

I said, "Did you know some of this creek, right here, will make it all the way to Mexico?"

She straightened, looking at me like I was teasing her again.

"Honest. Gus told me. Yesterday at the library, I checked it out on the map. It's true!"

Peering back over the edge, she said to that water, "Tell my family I love them."

35

"Ouch!" Tom cried as Perla's little blue Parcheesi man captured his red one, sending it back to the start.

Gus and Tom had taught her how to play while I helped Mom clean up the dinner dishes (and snuck a pillow from the hall closet to my other bed). Right from the start Perla hardly ever counted out her steps along the board. Instead she moved her men in jumps, according to its pattern. Strategy seemed a snap for her, and I could see why she'd earned the Excellence in Math award.

"Yow!" Gus cried as she captured one of his yellow men and sent it back to the start with a smile like an apology.

Her little man reminded me of the map's long blue line, and before I knew it I'd said, "Gus, could a person float all all the way to Mexico on the Colorado River?" I turned hot all over.

Gus glanced at Tom, who kept his face still in that knowing-stuff way. Glancing at Mom, he cleared his throat. "Funny you should ask: I've been researching that exact question on and off for a few years. I've been wanting to make that journey for an adventure. It won't be easy. From its headwaters in Rocky Mountain National Park to the Gulf of California, the river stretches 1,450 miles. There's eleven dams before it reaches the sea. Closest I can figure, floating the whole distance will take a little over three months. Recently they've started to let water out of dams upriver, into the Colorado River Delta, but—"

"What's *that*?" I asked, relieved he thought I meant a raft.

"A *delta*? You know what a delta is."

"No, I don't," I said, like *Duh?*

"It's a place where a river flows into standing water—an ocean, or a lake. Sand or silt builds up in a triangle shape, forming the delta. Some deltas are small. Some are huge. This one is huge, but there's hardly even a trickle of water left flowing into the gulf."

"What?" I glanced at Perla, who was acting like she wasn't listening, but obviously was. "How?" I rolled the dice and moved one man forward.

"The Colorado River provides water to cities—Phoenix, Las Vegas, Los Angeles. It provides water for drinking and cooking and showers and farms and lawns and golf courses and swimming pools and electricity. It provides so much water that it gets all used up."

"Ha!" I said.

"Huh?" Gus said.

Perla captured another one of Gus's men, one that'd almost made it home safe.

"Unbelievable!" Gus cried. "You've really never played Parcheesi before?"

She shook her head, then counted two spaces and leapt her man up the home stretch to win. Gus and Tom looked at each other in shock.

"Gosh, Perla," I said. "You're a prodigy!"

She was smiling so big and I tried to smile back, but I missed Dad so danged much that it came out all crooked.

Night was slinking in, turning the sky my favorite color. Gus and Tom put Parcheesi away.

Act normal, act normal, I told myself, but then my danged mouth blurted, "So floating all that way to Mexico is impossible?"

"You'd have to portage a lot," Gus said.

"'Portage' means carry your boat," I explained to Perla.

"It'd be easier to ride a bike," Tom said.

"But not nearly so cool," Gus said.

"Speak for yourself!" Tom winked at me.

"Yeah!" I agreed.

"Pedalers not paddlers!" Tom raised a fist.

That was *exactly* what I needed just then, so, lifting high onto one knee on the bench, I raised my own fist and announced, "Pedalers not paddlers!"

Glancing up from her newspaper at my belly peeking out, Mom smiled. "That shirt's getting too small for you." She sounded glad about it.

I plopped down, tugging on the hem.

Eyes on her newspaper, she said, all casual, "You don't like rivers, Rill?"

How—after what'd happened to Dad—could she even *ask* that question? Both my hands pulled to fists. My sore knuckles whispered, *Stop! Stop!* but my mouth grumbled, "I hate rivers!" *Stop!* I told myself, but out spilled, "They're double-crossers! Betrayers! They steal things and…and…" That awful picture of Dad in the rapids filled me, clear into my fingers and toes. "AND NEVER GIVE THEM BACK!"

Mom's breath snagged.

The muscle in Gus's jaw jumped.

I sprinted to my bedroom.

I buried my face in my pillow to push away that picture of Dad in churning water at the canyon's bottom. But it stayed. I cried. Cried like I'd never cried before. Cried so much my eyes ached and my face seemed to melt.

"Meow?" Clifford said, real gentle. He pressed my arm with his paws, but I didn't look up. Everything I'd been holding inside since the day Dad left came gushing out.

When I finally felt empty, I lifted my head. And there was Perla's braid. She sat on the floor, leaning back against the bed, staring at that mural.

"I know this sad," she said.

I sat up, eyes stinging.

"Your father, *he* painted this, yes?"

"Yes," I whispered. Then—even though it seemed impossible—I started crying again.

"Our fathers painted for us," she said.

"Yes," I whispered.

"Your father, he is gone?"

"Yes."

"Forever?"

"Yes." It was barely a word.

She looked at her crossed legs. "In a river?"

"Yes."

"That night, when the Immigration came, Papá, he opened the window. I climbed out. He said, 'I will come back for you!' But maybe he never will."

We listened to that danged creek rub it in.

"We are friends with fathers gone," Perla finally said.

"Gone," I whispered.

When I woke up, Perla was dressed and sitting on the floor, looking through the photo album from my shelf. Dad and I'd made that album. Opening it without him had seemed like cheating, so ever since he'd been gone, I'd left it on the shelf. I wanted to shout, "GET OUTTA THERE!" Except Dad wasn't coming home. Ever. I understood that now.

I flopped back on my bed, staring at the ceiling. "Have you been up a long time?" Sore was everywhere—my eyes, my knuckles, my legs.

"Always, I wake up early. Before school, I sell tamales to the other houses. For the lunches."

"Really? Even here they made you work before school?" All I did most mornings was fight with Eddy.

Perla shook her head. "It is good. We make money."

When Perla and I sat down to breakfast, I expected Eddy to call us dorks or babies. But he didn't. He didn't even look at us while he chewed his cereal.

Mom came over and petted my hair. "What are you girls doing today?" It was her guest voice, but her eyes were almost as puffy as mine, and she seemed deep-down sad.

"I'm teaching Perla to arm-wrestle and shoot my slingshot."

"That sounds fun," Mom said. "Eddy, could Perla borrow your slingshot?"

I expected a cranky answer, but he just shrugged and said, "Sure." He glanced at me, then away.

Do you ever wonder why, that day, Dad didn't just stay away from the edge? I mean, it's what he would've told us to do. I could see the words floating in the air between us.

Did Gus look sad this morning too? And Joyce? Probably. It was all my fault: I was making everyone miserable. Except Perla. She was munching and smiling. "This cereal is good, Ms. Kruse," she said.

"Well, thank you, Perla," Mom said.

After Mom, Eddy, and Gus left for the day, and after Joyce filed away all the signed waiver forms, Perla learned to arm-wrestle. We stood at Joyce's special table that she kept under the high cupboards for camping gear.

Bracing her legs, Joyce rested her right elbow on the table's pad, just so. Her right palm was up, and her left arm lay flat along the edge, gripping the peg for balance. I stood on the wooden box Dad made for me and rested my elbow, just so. Putting my left arm flat, I gripped the peg the way Joyce did. We gripped right hands, and Joyce showed Perla how to snap her wrist and surge forward, lightning fast, with her whole body. It made all my sore places shout, but it calmed my raw insides. Joyce let me win a couple times, but she and Leo were the only people I could not beat.

Perla climbed onto the box, and Joyce helped get her elbow in the right spot, helped lay her arm down just so and grip the peg.

"But you are so fast!" Perla gave us a nervous smile.

Then Joyce gripped Perla's hand, saying, "Ready…go!" Joyce took it easy on her, but for a beginner, Perla did pretty good. Still, she wasn't like me. This was a place where I *never* got mixed up.

"Maybe Gus should make another box, so you and Perla can practice on each other!" Joyce said.

I looked at Perla. She nodded.

After lunch I led her into the meadow behind home.

"Grip the slingshot this way." I took it in my hand how Dad had taught me, but then there he was again, lying in that water. I sagged. Perla rested her hand on my shoulder till the picture went away. I cleared my throat.

"Put the rock in the leather part, like this. Hold your front arm straight, and pull back till your other hand is even with your cheek. Aim down the *V*." I aimed at the faded lid from a yogurt container, which Dad had nailed to a tree for me to shoot at. He was always putting up new lids because I shot them to shreds. I'd been carrying my slingshot around, but I hadn't actually shot in forever, so this lid was still there. It was one of the last things he'd done for me, and I didn't want to ruin it.

But Dad would hate that I hadn't been shooting. The Stingray, my photo album, this slingshot—I hadn't been doing all these things I loved because of him. I was trying to keep life exactly like it was the day he left, but it was changing anyway. And if he were here, I knew he'd scold me. All of a sudden I saw the Rill I'd been since he'd left, plain and clear. A Rill that wasn't really me. But without Dad, who was I supposed to be?

Taking a deep breath, I shot. The rock thwacked against the lid.

"Amazing!" Perla loaded a rock into Eddy's slingshot. She aimed and shot. Instead of a thwack there was nothing. She tried again. And again. She never did hit the lid, but she did hit the tree next to it once.

"Take this slingshot when you go back to Fort Kruse tonight. That way you'll have it if you're scared."

Perla shook her head. "I have my 'Ready…go!'" She tried the lightning-fast motion she'd learned from Joyce. "Like you with Tate! And I have this." She touched Eddy's whistle at her chest. I realized then that he must've noticed she wore it. But he hadn't said a word.

Would I hear Perla blow on that whistle in the night? I decided yes, but after what I'd done to Tate, after the things I'd said to Mom, Gus, and Eddy, I knew *I* was the most dangerous thing Perla could meet.

38

A week went by. Each morning I'd ride over to fetch Perla. We'd say hi to Sir Charles, then we'd ride to my house. After a few days, I stopped expecting flashing lights to cross the bridge and Sheriff Willisden to march into the lobby of Kruse Whitewater Adventures. I never forgot that fuming that'd taken me over, though. Calling rivers "thieves" also lurked around each day, especially when Gus or Mom looked at me. Eddy looked at me different too. I tried to ignore it all. I just wanted to move on. Besides, it was Perla I needed to worry about. Perla faced a *way* bigger problem. Each day we'd check the mail, and each day there was no letter. "It'll come," I'd say to her, but I was starting to doubt that.

One afternoon she said, "On a bicycle I could find my family?"

"Maybe." I shrugged. "But we don't know where they are. Your dad promised he'd come back. He will."

One morning, petting Sir Charles, she said, "On a horse I could find my family?"

I shrugged. "Your dad promised he'd come back. He will."

One afternoon, as I read *Chitty Chitty Bang Bang*, Perla said, "In a flying car I could find my family."

"Yep." But *I* didn't want a flying car anymore. Didn't need one.

Gus built that second wooden box, so we practiced arm wrestling. I took it easy on her, but she also got pretty good. She never got very good with the slingshot. What she was good at was singing. Once she was comfortable being at Kruse Whitewater Adventures, she sang when she walked, sang when she drew stuff, sang when she played Parcheesi, sang when she ate lunch, sang when she arm-wrestled, sang when she shot the slingshot, sang when she rode on the back of the Stingray.

"You're the singin'-est girl I've ever seen!" Joyce said one day.

Perla taught me songs. One, called "Las Mañanitas," she said Mexicans sang at birthdays and special times. She taught me the Mexican national anthem. She taught me "Cielito Lindo," that first song she'd sung. I loved to belt out the *"ay, ay, ay, ay"* part. My singing was scratchy and awful, but Perla's was so clear and pretty. Still, I didn't care because—like with reading—it was just us two.

My favorite song was "La Cucaracha." I'd heard it before at school and assumed it was just a game. Like the chants when we jumped rope. But in Mexico, Perla told me, it was a traditional song. An important song that everybody knew. Its beginning went "*La cucaracha, la cucaracha,*" which meant "the cockroach, the cockroach." I could not believe there was an important song about a nasty old bug, but Perla insisted it was true. The song's eight lines told how the cockroach lost one of its legs but limped on. Its rhythm, she explained, matched that limp. Right after she said that, our eyes locked, because we understood how that felt.

We started singing "La Cucaracha" all the time. We'd make up our own words. Goofy stuff, usually. Hilarious stuff, sometimes, that made us laugh till we doubled over. Each time I bent over laughing, though, I could feel something bubbling inside. Something down deep. Something bigger, stronger, and scarier than anything I'd faced before.

39

On Saturday afternoon Perla and I were hanging around on the banks of the creek. I hadn't been to that spot since the first day of summer vacation, but she'd wanted to walk out the trail. Lying back in the cool grass, I took in the wide sky. Understanding Dad was gone hurt so bad. But it also felt right. Which made me feel guilty. And that made me cranky. In fact, each day—even though I'd been cramming it deep in my belly—I was getting crankier and crankier.

Clifford climbed onto me, purring. I pushed him away. He stood there a minute, giving me a dirty look, so I gave one back. Flicking his tail, he walked into Perla's lap.

I crinkled my nose at that water beside us, so rude and loud. I hated it more than ever. Except…the water Dad scouted, from up on those cliffs, must've been *way* bigger and *way* louder.

Do you ever wonder why, that day, Dad didn't just stay away from the edge? I mean, it's what he would've told us to do.

With a jolt I realized it was one week till my birthday. Father's Day usually fell on the Sunday before, which meant it was *tomorrow*. But nobody'd said a word about it. Same as last year. Probably nobody would ever talk about Father's Day ever again.

Then…*bam!* All that crankiness broke loose and shot straight to my skull. I was boiling mad, but not at Mom, Eddy, Gus, or Joyce. No, I was furious at *Dad*.

He should've been more careful!

The grass and flowers rose tall around me. Sitting up, I yanked out a blossom, roots and all. Crinkling my nose, I popped off its head with my thumb, then crumpled the stalk

in my fist. He should have known better! *This* was what had
been bubbling down deep. And *this* was worse—way worse—
than when I'd shouted at Whitney in the fort. Worse than
when I'd shouted *SHUT UP!* at Eddy. Worse than when I'd
shouted at Gus. Worse than when I'd jumped off the porch
swing and shouted at Mom. Worse than when I'd shouted at
rivers in front of everyone. Worse than when I'd punched
Tate Willisden. I flopped back in the grass, then rolled over,
groaning, and buried my face.

"Rill?" Perla said.

My mouth took over. "Your parents were *dumb!*" Even
though I wasn't moving, I breathed hard as a train. I pushed
my forehead into the ground, listening, but Perla didn't make
a peep. After a while I rolled over and hung one arm across
my face. From underneath I peeked at her.

She sat with her legs and arms crossed, watching me with
knife eyes. Clifford sat in her lap with his front paws crossed,
too, and the same sharp expression. I remembered how mad
Perla got when I'd said things about her family before, but I
couldn't care. I was too furious.

At Dad.

Then Perla sang, like "La Cucaracha":

I knew a river,
It stole a father,
And his daughter
She was mad.

But her father,
Was the one who,
Made the danger
Choice so bad.

"Take it back!"

"It is the truth, yes? This is why you hate the river? This is
why you say mean things about *my* family?"

I was on my feet in a snap, towering over her. "My dad

died! At least your dad's *alive!* But then again," I could not stop my mouth, "MAYBE HE'LL NEVER COME BACK! MAYBE HE MIGHT AS WELL BE DEAD TOO!"

Perla's eyes tangled, and then she slumped like I'd punched her. She hugged her knees. Clifford squeezed out with his ears pressed flat against his head.

I marched away, but her stupid song kept repeating in my head, making me even more furious. After ten steps I stopped to shout, "SHUT UP!" at the sky. But that song kept going, pressing all around me. Turning back, desperate, I flung out my arm at Perla, at Dad, at the river, at the whole stupid world. "GIVE ME A BREAK!"

Storming for home, part of me thought, *Go back! Tell her you're sorry!* But I couldn't.

Even though I avoided the lobby, Joyce stepped out its side door, giving me a once-over. "Someone sure churned up the mud in your pool! Where's Perla?"

"WHO CARES!"

I stomped up the metal stairs to the deck, slammed my bedroom door, and plopped on the first bed. I did not lie down. I did not cry. Instead I curled my lip at that girl in her pink nightgown, riding that unicorn into the clouds. I couldn't see her face, only her hair streaming in the wind, but I knew she wore a huge grin. Just then I hated that girl. Hated that whole stupid mural. I even—no, *especially*—hated Dad.

"Meow?" Clifford called from outside the door.

I grabbed my backpack and fished out my slingshot, imagining Dad showing me how to shoot. *Put the rock in this leather part, like this. Now, hold your front arm straight, and pull back till your other hand is near your cheek. Aim down the* V. Aiming right at the butt of that girl on the unicorn, I shot. The rock thwacked, leaving a little white hole. I imagined Dad's breath snagging. It felt so good. Loading another rock, I shot her in the shoulder. It thwacked again, leaving another little hole. I heard his breath snag again. I loaded another rock and shot her in the hand that gripped the unicorn's mane. Another thwack. Another hole. Another snagged breath. I shot her in the back of the head. Because that mural was Dad's promise of how my life was supposed to be.

And he'd broken that promise.

40

The next morning I sat across from Eddy, all grumpy in my nightgown as I poured a bowl of cereal. Clifford cleaned himself in a living room chair, all grumpy too. With me. The screen door clapped behind Mom as she left. She needed to help run the lobby since Joyce had a rare day off.

I was still mad about Perla's song, but all my energy had drained away, and I was caught in my own swirling thoughts. I didn't even realize Eddy'd sat back and was watching me with his arms crossed. When I finally did notice, I said, "What?" with my mouth full.

His face had an expression I'd never seen. Not mad. Not plotting to make me mad. No, it was calm and firm. And instead of spitting out "baby" or "dork," he seemed to be weighing his words. "It's Father's Day," he said.

I swallowed hard on my cereal.

"I've been thinking about what you asked," he said. "About Dad. About why he'd stand close enough to the cliff's edge to fall into the river."

I tried to swallow again, but a lump blocked my throat.

But her father,
Was the one who,
Made the danger
Choice so bad.

"I spent a couple days thinking you were right. I mean, why *would* he take a risk like that? One he'd warn *us* back from? I got really, really mad for a while. But then I realized Dad was there to kayak a ridiculously dangerous section of big water. He was looking for the safest route." Eddy snorted. "Like there could even *be* a safe route. He could just as easily have died kayaking that section. So then I spent a while really, really mad at him for kayaking in the first place. I was mad at Gus, too, for taking him there. For the way they'd always egg each other on."

Eddy ran his hand across his forehead and I remembered Dad used to do that. "They were scouting out the headwaters of the Colorado River, did you know? For an adventure Gus was planning. I got even madder about that."

Pressing his palms on the table, he concentrated on the backs of his big, skinny hands. Red streaked up his neck and into his face. "Then, a couple nights ago, it came to me that Dad was just being himself. And if he hadn't loved to do those dangerous things, he wouldn't have been Dad. He wouldn't have been the dad we knew. Does that make sense?" Eddy looked right at me with eyes like lasers.

I tried to nod, but I was frozen in his stare with that lump clogging my throat and a burning frown.

"The dad we knew was awesome." He stood, grabbing his bowl and glass. "And I wouldn't want him any other way." He clinked them into the dishwasher. The screen door clapped behind him.

I stared at the raisins and flakes floating in the white. There was a plop into the milk, and I realized it was my own tear. That lump crept down my throat to my chest and squeezed. It felt like when I squeezed the kitchen sponge. Except this lump squeezed way, way harder. It pulled and pulled, until everything inside me scrunched to a knot. Even my heart. It hurt so bad.

Hunching forward, I rocked. I shut my eyes. I rocked more and whimpered and hunched even more.

"Meow?" Clifford said from beside my chair.

But I couldn't open my eyes. I could barely breathe.

I worried my heart would stop beating. I worried I'd die from the pain. I worried I'd turn into nothing but that knot.

It lasted forever and forever and forever.

And then it finally stopped.

I felt dizzy. My chest seemed to unfurl. Sipping a long breath, I sat up straighter. Another tear plopped down, onto the edge of the table. There against the wood, it reminded me of that lonely guitar. *Sing and do not cry.* Perla sang all the time.

I shot up so fast my chair banged to the floor behind me. I jogged to my bedroom and stood facing that mural, blinking at the holes I'd made. I studied every detail Dad had painted. There was our big brown building, with Mom sitting on her deck swing. There was the trail leading across the meadow, then into the trees and around the cliffs to Fort Kruse. There was its *K* flag lifted on a breeze. There was the trail along the creek bank. In the creek was a place where the water curled around a rock and curved back on itself: an eddy. On one of the mountains, a thin blue line moseyed down to a brook: a rill. High above, an eagle soared in the sky. Of course that girl was grinning. How could she not?

I studied her hand gripping the unicorn's mane. I traced the hole I'd made there. I traced the hole on her butt. Reaching up, I touched the one on her shoulder. I stood on tiptoes to reach the hole on her head. Copying how her hand gripped the mane, I pressed my own hand there and imagined I was her.

"Dad?" my voice was croaky. "I miss you so much." My bottom lip was all over the place, but I went on. "I just wish you hadn't been so dumb!" I pressed my forehead against the mural to steady myself. "I guess I make mistakes too." I hiccupped and laughed at the same time. "Actually, I'm the worst. I've been spreading 'sorry' everywhere! I make dumb choices I don't understand, or even realize I'm making. I think I'm doing the right thing when really I'm being *such* a dork." I wiped my nose on my sleeve. "I get why you painted this now. It's how you hoped my life would turn out. Right? Like Perla's dad singing to her?" My voice went high and thin. "Except you're not here!" It took everything I had to clear my throat and go on. "It's okay, though, that you made that mistake. I guess we all mess up." Then, for once in my life, the right words came: "I forgive you."

I stayed that way for a long while and, you know, my guts calmed in a way I hadn't felt since that last ordinary Monday when Dad kissed me on the top of my head, then left through the screen door for good.

Clifford weaved between my legs, purring.

I realized my palm pressed the mural the same way Eddy's had pressed the table, that my face held the same expression. *Eddy.*

I jogged out the screen door and down the stairs. I rushed alongside the building and through the door into the garage. He'd already finished packing up the sandwiches and drinks.

The guests crowded the lobby. Nudging through them, I saw Mom watching me, all puzzled. As I reached the front door, a man guest yelped. A lady guest said, "For heaven's sake, Burt, it's just a cat!"

Eddy stood at the back of a van, loading sandwiches into a big cooler. I ran straight into him with a hug. He froze with his arms out like wings. After a minute, sighing, he hugged me back.

41

Later that morning I hurried along the trail to Fort Kruse, Clifford loping behind. When I got there, the shutters were closed. The *K* flag floated on a soft breeze. I climbed the ladder and lifted the trap door. Perla was gone, but her sack bulged with her things on the table.

Beside it were three drawings she must've made the night before. One was of her bright blue trailer with the crabapple tree, the tiny garden with the yellow tulips, and the river flowing by across the road. The second was of a tan house with a river behind it. Next to the house was part of a stable with a horse. On its other side stretched a green field. Perla's two homes. The third picture looked like the cover of *Chitty Chitty Bang Bang*, except there were two rows of back seats with a bigger girl and boy in one and a smaller girl and boy in the other. Perla and Pablo. All their arms were lifted and they wore open smiles.

Obviously, she'd left early for the stables.

I sprinted back along the trail to home. I rushed into the garage, got the Stingray, and stopped to tell Deena, the part-time girl, Joyce's cousin, where I was headed. I asked her to hold Clifford. Deena grabbed him, sat down in Joyce's chair, and went back to reading her magazine.

I pedaled across the bridge, turned right onto the two-lane highway, and rode as fast as my legs would go. Just before I got to the road to the stables, I spied red, way ahead—a red dress with a dark braid.

Town was pretty close when I caught up to Perla. Passing her, I slammed on the brakes so the back wheel did a one-eighty. "Where are you going?"

She kept right on walking in her brown shoes.

Steering the bike around, I hustled until I walked beside her. "Aren't you talking to me?"

She shot me a dirty look. Her jaw was set, and it took few seconds before she said, "To church."

"Church? Aren't you scared?"

"Yes."

"Aren't you afraid of Immigration? Couldn't you get caught?"

Perla shrugged. "If I am caught, then I will go to my family on the bus."

"But what if they're still here? Or on their way back?"

Perla shrugged again. "You said they will not come back."

"Yeah...um...that was mean. I'm really, really sorry. You were right. So right. I was mad at my dad. I shouldn't have said those things to you. Lately, I can get *so* mad, and I can't stop myself. But I'm gonna try. You're my best friend. And I don't want you to get caught!"

Caught. Town wasn't far ahead. *Tell her Maria Her- says she can stay with her! Tell her she can stay with Norma Jim-!* Now I'd get caught in my own lies, and Perla would get caught by Immigration. Oh, I'd done so many things wrong!

Perla kept walking.

I said, "Your dad promised he'd—"

"I KNOW WHAT HE PROMISED!"

Awkward quiet elbowed in between us.

In a little voice, Perla finally said, "Maybe you said the truth. Maybe he will *never* come back."

"Perla, I really am sorry—"

"I don't want sorry! From you! From him! I want my family!" She walked faster. With the Stingray it was hard to keep up.

"Okay...do you want a ride then?"

She stopped, eyes flashing. "I FEEL!" She poked her chest with her finger. "*I FEEL!*"

"I know."

"No! You know nothing! For you, I am only a girl from Mexico! A thing to keep you from feeling sad!"

"No—" There I was, lying again. I owed Perla honesty. "Well, I guess you were at first...just Mexican, I mean. And the keeping-me-from-sad-thing." I remembered us standing there, me with the stick ready to swing, Perla with her hands and chin lifted. "But didn't *I* seem like just a mean old white girl to you?" I remembered her stepping out from behind that tree, wiping her tears on her jeans. "Oh, jeez! It doesn't matter! Because all that's changed! I got to know you! And you got to know me! We're *friends* now! In fact you're the *best friend* I've ever had! And you helped me understand important stuff!"

She sighed. Then she seemed to actually see me. "You look bad."

"I do?"

"Very bad."

I noticed the ratty jean shorts and wrinkly old T-shirt I'd scooped up off the floor. I'd dressed in such a hurry, I hadn't paid any attention to what I'd put on. My hair wasn't in its pigtails or even brushed. The breeze tickled a piece of it across my face, but I didn't budge.

Perla sighed again. "Okay. I will ride."

42

The church was one of the oldest buildings in town. On a history field trip in third grade, I'd learned it was built in the 1890s and its marble floors came from a quarry up the railroad line. That quarry mined the same marble for the floors of the state capitol. The church had arches across its entrance and a tower with a bell that rang through town every hour.

All my life I'd heard that bell. I'd hear it as I ran on the playground at school, or as I strolled into the grocery store or the post office. I'd gotten so used to hearing it, I'd stopped thinking of it as coming from the church. It was just part of being in town. Now I frowned up at its tower. Each ring seemed to scold *Caught! Caught! Caught!*

We climbed off the Stingray. Cars and people were everywhere. Perla walked slower now. Her eyes were scared, but she held her chin high. I tried to do the same.

"Well, hello, Rill!" said a shaky voice.

It was Mrs. John from the post office. She wore a bright green pantsuit and a necklace of yellow beads like gumballs with a silver cross. On her feet were shoes with big silver buckles. I'd never seen Mrs. John's feet because she always stood behind the post office counter. It was weird to see her feet. I'd also never seen her hair outdoors. It seemed more purple than white.

"Isn't this a fine day?" Her eyes rested on Perla. Before I could answer, her gaze lifted over our heads. "Good morning, Frank!"

We hustled to the wide walkway leading to the church, which had a fancy marble fountain smack its middle.

"Oh, hello! Look, dear, it's two of our favorite students!"

There stood Mr. Rainey. Beside him, with her hand hooked through his arm, was Ms. Márquez. I tried not to stare at her belly, but sure enough, there was a bump from a baby.

"*Hola,* ladies!" Ms. Márquez said. "I'm glad to see you returning to Mass, Perla. And you've brought Rill! That's so nice!" Her words were light and friendly, but her eyes said all sorts of serious stuff to Perla.

Perla looked back at her for a few breaths, then down.

Ms. Márquez said, "I have something for you. Can you wait a minute?"

I glanced around—on the lookout for Immigration—but Perla nodded.

Pulling her hand from Mr. Rainey's arm, Ms. Márquez started away, but he said, "I'll get it. You stay and chat." They shared a knowing-stuff look before he left.

She smiled at us. "How have your summers been so far?"

"Fine," I said.

"I heard you visited the library. Have you done other fun things?"

Perla and I glanced at each other. "We've just been hanging out," I said.

Ms. Márquez's gaze leapt to Perla. Worry seemed to take over her face.

Mr. Rainey hustled up, holding something behind his back.

Ms. Márquez said, "Perla, I put this in the car for Mr. Rainey to give to you if he saw you at the library. I'm so glad to see you today because I wanted to present it to you myself." Ms. Márquez's eyes turned watery. "You certainly earned it. You are one of the brightest, hardest-working students I've ever taught."

Mr. Rainey handed her a rectangle of thick creamy-colored paper, and she held it out to Perla. Around the outside was a fancy gold border. In its middle, big black letters announced EXCELLENCE IN MATH. Below that, in blue, was PERLA

INFANTE. There was the school's seal, and beside that Ms. Márquez had signed it, along with Principal Walker.

Perla just stared at that award. I nudged her, and she accepted it from Ms. Márquez, who crouched down and hugged her, saying things in Spanish into her ear. Then she rested both hands on Perla's shoulders and they looked at each other. Really looked. Ms. Márquez nodded and Perla nodded back.

It made me uncomfortable, so I glanced up at Mr. Rainey. He was smiling down at *me* with shining eyes.

Ms. Márquez stood—kind of awkward on account of the baby—then hooked her hand back through Mr. Rainey's arm. They strolled around the fountain, headed for the church's entrance. Perla watched them till they disappeared inside.

I asked, "What did she say?"

"She said she came to my First Communion."

First Communion was what the pretty white dress was for. "That's nice."

"I was not there."

"Seriously? Why?"

"The night before, the Immigration took my family."

43

I'd never been to church. *Better to be in the wilderness thinking about God, than in a church thinking about the wilderness,* Dad always used to joke. Even his memorial service was held in just an outdoor theater. Except for the vases of flowers on either side of the front doors, being in this church sure felt different. It was different from a field trip too.

Perla found us seats on one of the long wooden benches near the back. The rest of the church was full. A man in black robes strode like a king to a little stage. I decided he was the priest, especially when he started talking about forgiveness. He had a nice voice, a deep voice. He read for a bit, then led everybody in a prayer, and after, they all moved their hands over their chests in the same pattern, saying, "Amen."

At first I listened. It got me thinking about how I'd forgiven Dad for dying, and I felt so sad. But also right. I thought of the priest at Perla's church in Mexico, who spoke out against the bad men, so they killed him. Truth probably meant more to her than it would to other people. My lying would seem awful when I finally fessed up about the ladies. I crossed my fingers that this priest's message about forgiveness would help.

Caught! Caught! Caught!

I searched for people I knew in the benches. Maria and Norma especially. I had to lean all over to see around the adults. It was also hard to recognize people from behind.

Perla elbowed me and gave me a dirty look.

I tried to sit still.

Someone wore lots of perfume, making me wave in front of my nose to get fresh air. Since I couldn't see much, I looked at the ceiling. Its big arches reminded me of a whale skeleton in a museum. Light streaming through high windows danced around up there, and it seemed a place where angels might hang out. I wondered if it looked like heaven.

Closing my eyes, I thought of all the important stuff I'd learned since meeting Perla. I opened my eyes—and this'll sound crazy—but I imagined myself zooming around those high arches on that unicorn. An eagle soared beside me. All the hard things I'd learned since meeting Perla floated up there, and, steering the unicorn by its mane, I pierced each one with its horn till I collected them all.

Everybody stood to sing, so I shot to my feet. As Perla sang, she looked so happy, yet also sad. Her voice joined with all those others, lifting to that ceiling. It sounded beautiful. Powerful. It reminded me of the creek. Which made me think of Dad again, and suddenly I felt him. There was his sunny-shirt smell as his arm wrapped around my shoulders and he smiled down. He wasn't nearly so tall. Or, no, that wasn't it: *I* was taller, and I knew this memory was from now. The song ended. Everybody sat down.

Mounted on the back of the bench in front of us was a rack with Bibles in it. On one side of the rack was a slot with little envelopes. On the other was a slot with stubby pencils. I took an envelope and a pencil. The front of the envelope read My Offing. *Offing?* Looking again, I saw *Offering.* Below that was Name with a blank line. Below that was Amount with a line. I still didn't get what the envelope was for, but I wrote *Deer Perla* on the Name line. Then, on the Amount line, I wrote *I made a dum mistake. I'v bin keaping a seacret. Sum ladys sed you culd stay with them.* I flipped the envelope over to finish on the back. *I was scaird that if I told you, yood leev and not be my frend anymor. Sory!*

I handed the envelope to Perla. She read it. Then she frowned at me.

44

We walked out of the church into bright sunshine.

"Rill! I thought that was you!" Joyce wore a yellow dress. Her hair was out of its high ponytail and brushed into a neat curl around her shoulders. She stood next to a wrinkly man in a brown suit who was just as tall. Leo stood beside him in a pale blue suit.

"Papá," she said, "this is Rill. And her friend, Perla."

The man smiled at us and nodded, sort of shy.

"Hi, Th-rill." Leo winked at Perla.

This was Joyce's dad? And *she* looked…pretty? Seeing her this way felt weird, but I said, "Pleased to meet you."

Past Joyce, through the crowd, I spotted Tate Willisden. He wore nice pants and a collared shirt. His dad stood beside him, shaking someone's hand. Tate had a fading black eye, but his nose was still one big bruise. His gaze stabbed the sidewalk. Like he sensed me looking at him, it lifted and flicked to Perla, then back to me.

"Someone sure dragged you through a rapid!" Joyce said. "Are you all right?"

"*¡Perla, ay, amigita!*" a lady called.

Perla turned, cried out, and darted for the voice.

I couldn't see through the tall crowd, but Joyce's eyes followed her. Watching, her lips pressed to a line. Through the gaps in the bodies, I spied Perla hugging a lady, her award and my note on the little envelope smushed against the lady's back. The lady was not Maria or Norma. They stood to the side, smiling and wiping their wet eyes. Joyce's eyes slid back to me.

"Rill," she said, "where are Perla's parents?"

"Joyce, I'll tell you everything in a bit. Okay? I just need to do some stuff for a minute."

I'd planned to rush to Perla, but my legs carried me in Tate's direction, and before I could stop myself, I stood right in front of him. He took a step back and glanced at his dad. Sheriff Willisden was turned away, talking to two men.

"I'm not gonna to hit you," I whispered. "I just wanna say sorry. Perla's my friend, you know? Wouldn't you fight for your friend?"

He studied me.

"Wouldn't you?" I repeated.

His dad turned to us. "Well, Tate, who's your friend?"

Tate and I stared at each other with wide eyes. But then a miracle happened: We both smiled. Not big smiles, but smiles just the same.

"I'm Rill." I held out my hand.

"Hello, Rill." Tate's dad shook it. "I'm Sheriff Willisden."

"Pleased to meet you. I gotta go." I took off for Perla, searching the people still there.

But Perla was gone.

I looked down at my ratty shorts and wrinkly T-shirt. All my hurry this morning to find her, to tell her the truth, to finally set things right, had been for nothing.

45

"So, they deported the parents and left the child!" Joyce slapped her leg and looked out the passenger window with a disgusted expression. I'd never heard "deported" before, but I could guess what it meant.

Leo glanced at her across his truck's long seat. He looked down at me beside him with his eyebrows raised, then back at the highway leading to Kruse Whitewater Adventures. The Stingray was in the bed of his truck.

Staring out the window, Joyce said, "My parents came to America hidden under a load of avocados! I understand why Perla's family came!"

"They did?" I said. "You do?" She nodded. "Do you think she'll ever forgive me?" I asked.

"Hard to predict! She seems wise for a fingerling! I hope so!"

"Can you not tell Mom?" I said. "Or Eddy? Or Gus? I want to tell them myself. Please?"

Joyce looked at me sidelong. "Okay! I'll give you one day! Only one day, understand?"

"Can I have till tomorrow night?"

She sighed but nodded.

"There's something else. I got in a fight."

"Rill!"

"But he deserved it. He was saying awful things about Perla. I did just what you taught me: I snapped my wrist and shot forward with my whole body like lightning. And I really whooped him."

The corners of Joyce's mouth quivered. "Was it the Willisden boy?"

"Yeah. And I apologized."

Sipping a wide breath, she seemed to force herself to frown as she patted my leg.

I looked up at Leo. He was just plain smiling.

We came to the company sign and he turned left onto the dirt road.

"Wait!" I cried.

Leo stopped the truck.

"I forgot to fetch the mail yesterday."

"Don't I know it!" Joyce said. "You were so churned up, I decided to let it go!" She climbed out.

I scooched across the bench seat and out the door. Then I hugged her. At first she seemed surprised—the way Eddy'd been—but after a second, she hugged me back.

"I'll walk from here," I said. "Have a nice rest of your day off."

Leo hopped out, strode to the back of his truck, and banged down the tailgate, the sides of his suit jacket flapping on the breeze. He lifted out the Stingray and set it in the tall grass next to me. "Bye, Th-rill," he said out the window as he backed away. When Joyce's side came around, she called, "Just leave that stuff on my desk!" Reaching out, she gave me a thumbs-up.

I turned to the mailbox, opened its big creaky door, and gathered the letters. There were a bunch of them, so I sat beside the Stingray in the grass on the road's edge, flipping through the envelopes. About halfway I found one with a stamp that had *Mexico* written across the bottom and Spanish words along its sides. It was addressed to *Rill Kruse, Kruse Whitewater Adventures* in penmanship that looked like a first grader's.

46

It took me till the afternoon of the next day to wrestle up enough courage to face Fort Kruse with Perla gone. Standing near the top of the ladder, I traced Dad's waving handprints. When I pressed my hand to my own print, it disappeared, and I saw that I truly had grown. I lifted the trap door, let it bang open, and climbed in.

In the murky light, I made out Perla's sack, her three drawings, and the colored pencils. I wasn't in a rush like yesterday, so now I noticed Eddy's whistle, the LED headlamp, batteries, and nightlight-and-alarm clock on the table. Even though she was gone, I heard Perla singing. I heard her singing all the time now.

Opening the shutters, I blinked at The Eagle's View of home. I took in the cloud-crowded sky. Did Dad watch from up there? Was he watching me that minute?

Clifford clawed his way into the fort. Meowing, he jumped to the windowsill and tickled my nose with his tail till I petted him. "At least *you're* still here," I said, with a sigh.

Turning, I walked to the WELCOME HOME! drawing and tugged it free of the thumbtacks. I looked at the pretty white dress hanging from a nail on the wall. On the shelf was Perla's framed photo of her family, next to mine. Below the shelf leaned the stick I'd dragged up that very first day.

I gathered the sleeping bag and pillow from the hammock and set them by the trap door. Sitting on a stump chair, I put my colored pencils back in their bag. I made a neat pile of Perla's drawings, then tugged down the rest of mine, stacked them on top, and stored them all in the pad of paper. I loaded a bunch of the stuff into my backpack.

There were footsteps on the ladder. I slunk to the far wall. The stick, of course, leaned against the opposite wall. Whoever it was stopped just below the doorway, but all I could hear was that danged creek.

Clifford trotted over and peered down. "Meow!" he said, like *Come on up!*

Perla's head, then shoulders, inched through the doorway. She looked super serious. "I want my things."

Kneeling, I pulled the pad out of my pack and handed over her drawings. She took her family photo from the shelf and put it in her sack, on top of the rest of her clothes. She folded her pretty white dress and put it in the sack, too, on top of the new black shoes. She balanced the teddy bear on the tiptop. The sack was overflowing.

"I am *so* sorry," I said.

She shot me a dirty look.

"I know. I made a dumb mistake. All this time, you could've stayed with one of those ladies, taking showers and eating things besides sandwiches and—"

"You lied!" she said. "You lied, but worse is you think I am a *bad friend*!"

"I don't—"

"You think I would leave and not come back? *Friends do not do this!*"

"Well, aren't you leaving right now?"

She stomped her foot. "Because I am very mad!"

"Sorry. You're right. All last year—all those Fridays—Mr. Rainey never once drew my name from the Compassion Box. Honestly, I don't think my name was ever even *in* that box. I'm a dork, a baby. I'm dumb. I don't understand anything."

Perla blew out a sigh. "You are *not* dumb."

"I was going to bring your things to Norma at work. I was going to leave them with her today. Along with your letter."

"My letter?"

"It's in my bedroom. Do you want to come get it?"

47

I handed Perla the letter. We stood at the bottom of the stairs because she wouldn't come up to the apartment. Taking the envelope with both hands, she stared at it. She traced the penmanship on the address. She flipped it over and started to open it but stopped. She crinkled her nose at me. "*Adiós.*"

I wanted so bad to know what it said. I wanted to shout, "Show me! At least show me before you go!" But—for once—I had control of my mouth, so instead I just watched her walk away, the letter poking from her back pocket. Her drawings were in one hand and her sack was in the other.

I trudged up the stairs to the deck swing, plopped onto it, and watched gray clouds gobble the sky. Perla had a long walk to town. I hoped she wouldn't get caught in the rain.

Clifford hopped up beside me. "Well, that's the end of my adventure," I said to him. Right that minute Perla was leaving along our road to the highway, but she seemed farther away than those places we'd seen in the atlas.

"I wish Mom were here." Shutting my eyes, I imagined a new memory: Mom and me sitting together on my bed as I told her about Perla and Fort Kruse, about my fight with Tate Willisden, and about finally understanding that Dad was gone forever. About forgiving him.

"Rill?"

I lunged to the top of the stairs.

Perla stood at the bottom. Through a humongous frown, she said, "You want to read my letter?"

48

Perla set down her sack and drawings near the side door to the garage. Marching to the far edge of the dirt lot, she pulled the letter from her back pocket. Clifford trotted up, all grumpy because I'd launched him from my lap when Perla'd called.

A vanload of guests rumbled across the bridge, and Mom waved from behind the steering wheel. Eddy sat in the passenger seat. Blowing dust slapped us. Another van with Gus driving rolled onto the bridge.

With a frustrated noise, Perla marched off along the trail beside the creek. When she reached the spot where we'd fought, she put her back to the wind, slid her thumb under the corner she'd already lifted, and tore the envelope the rest of the way open.

Thunder rumbled as she pinched out a piece of notebook paper that matched the one she'd written her own letter on. She folded the empty envelope in half and tucked it into her back pocket. Like it might crack into a million pieces, she unfolded the letter. Just seeing the words made her laugh and wipe her wet eyes.

Clifford rubbed against my shins, so I picked him up, petting him to keep my hands busy and my mouth quiet.

"They are home." Perla was all choked up. "Pablo and Javier are very happy." She leaned closer to the paper. "Abuelo, he is sick." Her eyebrows pinched together. "Very sick." She held the letter closer. Her lips started moving as she read, and then she went all pale.

More thunder rumbled.

"What does it say?"

Still gripping the letter, she covered her face with her hands, dropped to her knees, and leaked coyote howls.

"Perla?"

The letter whipped in the wind as she rocked back and forth. I watched her, not sure what to do. Then I sank down. Careful, like she truly was a wild animal, I put my arms around her. Her crying was loud and terrible and the letter flapped against our faces.

A gust blasted through the trees, making us sway as it yanked the letter from Perla's grip.

"Ay!" She shot to her feet.

The wind lifted it, then swirled it out over the creek.

"Please no! Please no!" I whispered, but, sure enough, it drifted down, down, down, and that trickster water snatched it.

At first only the middle fold got wet because the outside folds were propped against each other, making a tiny white tent. It bobbed up and down, spun front to back, as it rode the current.

Perla scrambled along the bank, searching for a way to get to it. She stopped at two boulders that reached way into the creek. In low season they were nice for sitting on, but this time of year they were just bumps below churning water. She grabbed a stick.

"Perla, don't!" I started for her, but she stepped onto the first boulder. Her sneakers disappeared in rushing wet. She wobbled but found her balance. Her eyes fixed on her letter as it floated near the second boulder.

"Perla! Come back!"

She hopped onto the second boulder, and for a second she seemed all right. Until her arms spun like the hands of a clock. She leaned way back, then way forward. Still holding that stick, she fell, face-first, into the creek.

"PERLA!" I screamed.

She bobbed up, sputtering, and held her letter high with

one hand. The greedy creek dragged her to its middle, into the fast-flowing current.

I started for her but stumbled over a yowl and landed hard on my knees. "Clifford!" I scolded.

A silver glint caught my eye: my whistle! Pressing it between my lips, I blew. I sprinted for Kruse Whitewater Adventures, blowing and blowing on that whistle.

Gus, Mom, and Joyce rushed out of the lobby. Guests followed close behind. Gus got to me first.

"Perla! Perla fell in the creek!" I pointed upriver.

Mom was already climbing the ladder on the back of a van. Straps whizzed as she untied *Ducky*.

"Here!" Gus shouted.

She passed him the kayak. Joyce handed him a paddle and he sprinted upstream.

"What's happening?" Eddy jogged out from the garage.

Sobbing, I sprinted up the path, eyes searching that twisting water for Perla. Eddy was right on my heels.

"There!" He pointed at something bobbing along in the middle.

"Eddy?" I cried.

He crouched down so I could climb onto him piggyback. And there was Perla.

"Eddy," I said real soft, "her eyes are shut!" Then I wailed, "NO! NO! NO! HER EYES ARE SHUT!"

I hadn't actually seen anyone I loved in a river since the weekend before Dad died. Since we'd all rafted the confluence together.

Now Gus, wearing a dismal expression, steered *Ducky* alongside Perla. The current dragged them under the bridge. Hunching down, reaching at the same time, he grabbed her T-shirt. On the bridge's other side, he heaved her up across the front of the kayak. He had to lift her a few times to get her limp body balanced with a leg on each side and her back propped against his chest. As he paddled for shore, the muscles of his jaw jumped. The rest of him strained against the powerful water and Perla's dragging feet.

Clifford pressed his front paws on my knees and I realized my hands covered my mouth. I heard the guests crowded behind me.

Mom and Joyce met Gus at the bank. I started for them, but Eddy grabbed my shoulders—not mean, but gentle. "Wait!" he said.

As they carried Perla to fluffy grass, one of her limp arms hung down, and the letter fell out of her hand. I tore from Eddy and grabbed it.

Mom bent over Perla's mouth, listening. I knelt down across from her. Perla's skin was bright red with cold.

"She's not breathing!" Mom said.

Joyce hooked a finger through Perla's mouth. "Airway's clear!"

Mom placed a palm on Perla's chest, right over the word *Padres* on her T-shirt. Pressing her other palm on that hand, she counted aloud as she pushed down thirty times. When she stopped, Joyce tilted Perla's head back, pinching her nose. She pressed down on her chin, and Perla's mouth opened. Joyce breathed into her two times. Mom started pressing on Perla's chest again. When she finished, Joyce breathed into her again.

Eddy knelt down next to Mom. Clifford stood beside him. Gus walked up, his breaths still puffing. Crouching down behind me, he rested his icy hand on my shoulder. I coughed out a sob because all of Perla was that cold.

I thought of the church's whale skeleton ceiling, of the angels, of the things I'd collected on that unicorn's horn, of the powerful joined voices, and of Dad's warm presence. Looking at the sky, I whispered, "Please, don't let the water steal her too!"

Mom pressed on Perla's chest a third round.

Nothing.

She pressed on her a fourth round.

Nothing.

"Please, Dad!" I whispered.

Halfway through the fifth time, Perla's fingers twitched. She coughed. She coughed more, and Mom rolled her onto her side. She coughed out water and water and water.

Joyce sat her up, real gentle, and she stayed there, hugging her and rubbing her shivering back.

The guests clapped. They breathed sighs of relief and said, "Wow!" and "How did that happen?" and "The poor dear!"

Clifford stepped right into Perla's lap and stared up at her.

Rain started then, hard, but nobody moved. Not even the guests.

Perla looked across them all, then up to Joyce beside her. She looked at Mom, Eddy, Gus, Clifford, and, finally, me.

Biting my wobbly lip, I held out the letter. It shook, the way Perla did, in the pelting wet.

Her eyes lifted from that letter to me. Then her face

seemed to cave in. "I'm sorry!" she whimpered, and looked down.

I hunched forward till I could see her face. "I'm sorry, too, Perla."

She seemed embarrassed but took the letter and pressed it to her chest. "Thank you," she squeaked.

Joyce grunted.

Mom said, "Oh, sweetheart."

Gus said, "You're welcome."

I said, "Nah, Perla. Thank *you*, for not leaving me."

Biting her lip, she leaned over till our foreheads met.

EPILOGUE

Fort Kruse is crowded.

Mom, Gus, Tom, Joyce, and Leo seem giant after spending so much time here alone with Perla. Eddy is almost as tall as Gus but *way* skinnier.

I sit on one stump chair. Perla sits on the other, all shy after Eddy insists. Leo sets a vase of flowers on the table between us and goes to stand beside Joyce. Tom is tying balloons to the nail where Perla's white dress used to hang. Everybody settles on the floor. Tom picks his way around bodies and over legs to join Gus against the far wall. With all those legs, there's hardly any floor left. The balloons make the ceiling seem just as full.

At a ruckus on the ladder, Eddy about has a heart attack because he sits next to the doorway. Clifford climbs through. "Meow!" he says like *Okay everybody, I'm here!*

We all crack up.

"That's one *gato loco*!" Joyce says.

Clifford weaves right through everybody, then hops into my lap. He inspects the cake on the table. Mom baked it the evening before. Double-dutch chocolate with vanilla frosting. My favorite. And Dad's. A green-frosting Stingray is on top, in a circle of eleven orange candles.

"Oh no, you don't!" I pull Clifford back.

Behind the cake are presents. A couple of them—ones from Mom—look like they're probably new clothes.

"Okay, Perla!" Joyce says. "Let's hear that letter!"

Perla fishes it from the front pocket of her hoodie. The notebook paper is dried like the skin of a raisin. She unfolds it, real careful, and clears her throat.

"Dear Perla," she reads in English.

Mamá, Frida and I are home. We spent three days in a jail in the city. We spent two days on a bus to Mexico. It is sad but also good to be home. The fields are green with new corn and beans. The horses and dogs miss you. Abuelo misses you. We all miss you. Pablo the most.

I know I promised I would return, but things are changed. Abuelo is very sick. I need to stay to work the farm. What I am saying is I will not return. Not soon. Mamá wants to help Abuelo in his last days.

What should you do? You must stay! Stay and learn and grow. Make the life we hoped for you when we left Mexico. I wrote to Maria Hernandez. She likes you, and her husband was with us on the bus, so she is alone now also. When we have money, we will send Frida to you.

Please write to us. We think of you every minute with love. Her voice cracks on that last part.

Kisses and hugs, Papá

Nobody says anything for a bit, but in the distance The Coyote Choir starts up. Mom sniffles and wipes her eyes. I sniffle too.

"Thanks for reading us that, Perla," I finally say.

"We're here for you, kiddo!" Joyce says, and everybody agrees.

Perla looks embarrassed, so I reach around the cake and squeeze her hand. Mom crawls forward and lights the candles. We've had my favorite dinner on the deck: chicken drumsticks, Mom's homemade mac 'n' cheese, and *no* vegetables. Then we all hiked out here with headlamps and flashlights for coming back in the dark. Now the sky is streaked with sunset and the glowing candles make the fort feel homey.

"Perla," Mom says, "you have a song for Rill?"

Perla nods. She sets her letter on the table and puts her father's guitar in her lap. She's been resting at Maria's house, but she still looks worn out and pale. She runs her thumb across the strings a couple of times and then starts playing. I hadn't expected her to be good. I recognize "Las Mañanitas" right away.

Eddy catches my eye. He gestures that I look like a trout gulping water—not mean, just looking out for me—so I shut my mouth.

Perla starts singing, and it's so pretty. I realize somebody hung the rainbow HAPPY BIRTHDAY! she drew for me where Dad's WELCOME HOME! used to be.

On the song's second verse, Leo puts his arm around Joyce and rests his head on her shoulder, and they join in. I look at Eddy. His face is calm and firm, and he stares at his sneakers as he listens. Mom stares at our family photo on the shelf, and she seems sad but happy at the same time. Tom's eyes sparkle. Gus leans back against the wall with his forearms resting on his knees and his eyes closed. He wears the ghost of a smile, and he seems to listen to every note.

The song ends and Mom says, "That was beautiful, Perla!"

"Gosh, Perla, thanks," I say.

"A singin' prodigy!" Joyce says.

"*We'd* better sing quick," Eddy says. "Those candles are almost gone."

Everyone starts "Happy Birthday to You." Their joined voices fill the fort till the ceiling and walls must be bulging. I can't even hear that creek. I decide this singing is the awesomest thing I've ever heard. When they stop, I just sit there, still feeling that song in my fingers and toes.

"Well, make a wish, Rill," Eddy says.

I can't stop grinning at these people who love me. I look at Perla and know they'll take care of her too. But I also know Perla and I will take care of each other, because that's what friends do. Hearing the creek, I imagine a squiggly blue line connecting all our hearts. I look out the window and imagine that line reaching into the orange sky. Then I gather my wish: that Dad can see us all right now. That he knows we miss him bad and will never forget him, but that we're okay.

I shut my eyes and blow.

AUTHOR'S NOTE

In the mid-nineties I taught high school language arts. Each year students who were new to America turned up in my classes. Some of them were undocumented, yet I'd become a teacher to help anyone with a desire to learn. These students were a marvel to me because, despite knowing little, if any, English, and despite knowing few of the basics of daily life within the school, they managed to get by. Often admirably. Often while also working one or even two jobs after school.

Some mornings I'd walk through the school's front doors to discover a group of them gathered in the lobby, crying and comforting each other because a family member, or maybe a few, had been rounded up for deportation the day or night before. I tried to imagine how that must have felt: being left behind in a foreign country with no documentation and no family. Later, these students would be in my class, trying to concentrate, learn, and continue on. Their courage amazed me. When I started writing novels, I knew this was a story I would someday explore.

This is very much Rill's story of accepting her father's death and forgiving him for it. A story about understanding her own grief and loss. It's Rill's own grueling, internal adventure. Yet she has help. As in life, through her interactions with Perla—someone of a different background—Rill gains a new and broader perspective that fosters compassion, helping her to heal and grow. Moments when we meet people who are different from us—in nationality, in ethnicity, in spiritual belief, in social strata—define us. They have the potential to be among the most beautiful experiences available to us as human beings. And because Perla faces a similar grief and loss, this is also her story. Yet I didn't dare tell it from her perspective because I am not of that heritage.

So my former immigrant students helped me.

Perla's story, though she's younger, is a blend of their experiences, especially those of one student in particular. The nighttime crawl through the hole under the fence follows that student's journey almost word for word. The account of the farm, her parents' advice, her older sister not attending but wanting to go to school, her brothers left behind—all of it is rooted in that student's reality. And as I listened to this former student insist that Perla's parents would tell her to stay in America, my heart nearly broke. *The River Between Hearts* would not have been possible without this help, and because of that, half of this book's royalties will go to this person.

Those immigrant students are grown now. Like Norma— the maid Rill meets in the hotel—they've become citizens. They're receptionists in doctor's offices, landscape supervisors, bankers. To all of them, I say *thank you*, for helping me directly and indirectly write this book, but even more for the richness and diversity you have brought, and continue to bring, to my community and life.

Besos y abrazos.

GRATITUDE

Every book is an adventure, with twists and turns, tests and joys, and a variety of people accompany me on the journey. The students I mention in my Author's Note were with me for each step of this book's creation. Next, I must thank the Vail Public Library and its marvelous staff. I drafted the majority of the novel there, at a wide table looking out through tall windows upon Gore Creek (yes, it was beautiful). My readers during the book's development—Sue Staats, Liza Alrick, Dorothy Henderson, Beth Cooney, and Nicole Magistro—your insights smoothed my strides. Denise Vega, your wise suggestion altered the route of the story's end, leading me to discover a path that brought it full circle: thank you! Todd Mitchell, paddler of rivers, you are a master of the craft, and I give you full credit for the novel's marvelous title. At Fitzroy books: thank you, Jaynie Royal, for selecting this book as runner up for the Kraken Prize and offering a publishing contract, for having the grit to create a press that explores hard social issues no matter a reader's age. And Pam Van Dyk, for your rare editor's gift of knowing just how to ask the question that leads a writer to crafting even more depth into a story, again, much gratitude.

I have a confession: During the creation of this book, I quit the writing business. It just felt too darned hard. But Rill and Perla reeled me back. Through those girls, I discovered the true reason why I write. It made all the difference in my craft, and in my career.

As always, tremendous love and gratitude to Ross and Sydney, for their support and patience as together we flow along this river called *life*.

And lastly, Norma Aziz, thank you for your clarifying read of all things Mexican. Like Rill, I hope you can see us all, right now. That you know we miss you bad and will never forget you.